GUARDIAN

THE ALFURIAN CHRONICLES
BOOK 2

AARON HODGES

Proofread by Sara Houston
Illustration by Eva Urbanikova

ISBN: 978-0-9951422-5-1

ABOUT THE AUTHOR

Aaron Hodges was born in 1989 in the small town of Whakatane, New Zealand. He studied for five years at the University of Auckland, completing a Bachelors of Science in Biology and Geography, and a Masters of Environmental Engineering. After working as an environmental consultant for two years, he grew tired of office work and decided to quit his job in 2014 and see the world. One year later, he published his first novel - Stormwielder.

FOLLOW AARON HODGES...
And receive TWO FREE novels and a short story!
https://aaronhodgesauthor.com/newsletter

Book 1: Warbringer

Book 2: Wrath of the Forgotten

Book 3: Age of Gods

Book 4: Dreams of Fury

The Alfurian Chronicles

Book 1: Defiant

Book 2: Guardian

Book 3: Conquest

The Swords of Heaven and Hell

Book 1: Darkstrider

The Four Circles

Book 1: Help! My Wizard Mentor Had A Heart Attack And Now I'm Being Chased By A Horde Of Giant Spiders!

The Untamed Isles

The Path Awakens

PROLOGUE

Serena Levaanton, Alfurian Princess to the city of Goma, strode down the corridor of Light. She enjoyed how it warmed her translucent skin, its energies seeping into her flesh, restoring her strength. It wasn't quite the same as a proper meal, but it helped to sooth the pain of her recent injuries.

It also gave her a much needed kick of adrenaline.

Emerging from the Light, she turned onto one of the regular corridors that ran about the circumference of the Levaanton tower. A great wall of glass offered her a stunning view over the human city. The slums of Goma were far, far below, and partly concealed by the near-constant smog that hung about the rusted rooves and broken brick buildings.

For just a moment, she wondered at the resilience of the humans that dwelled below. What must it be like, to breathe that poisoned air each and every day? To drink the poisoned waters and consume the flesh of dead creatures...

Serena shuddered, glad she would never know such misery.

Still, unlike many of her brethren, she harboured hopes that one day humanity might join the Alfur in their gilded towers. Her father claimed it was too dangerous to expose humanity to so much Light, but Serena was not convinced.

Though after her encounter last week in the arena, she had to admit, she'd had her doubts.

A shiver touched her and she reached unconsciously for the wound the human had opened on her arm. Left by the human's Light, this was no ordinary injury. It resisted the administrations of her father's healers, so that even a week later, the fiery pain lingered.

It *was* healing though. That was more than she'd dared hope a week ago, when she'd lain helpless in the sands of the arena and looked up into the burning eyes of her foe. The human had had every reason to strike her dead. After-all, she'd shown no such mercy to the gladiators who'd come against her when she'd fought as Rotin. By rights, she should be dead.

Instead, the human had spared her.

So much for mindless beasts.

For Serena, that act had been proof she was right. That humans could be more than mindless beasts.

That one day they might join the Alfur in the skies.

If only she might convince her father of that.

But Aiden Levaanton reminded frustratingly set in his ways. To him, the human's ascendancy with the Light was proof his every fear had been correct. That the humans were a threat they could not ignore, one that might undo all the works of the Alfur.

Serena paused in the corridor, coming to a stop outside a pair of finely wrought steel doors. An impossibly complex pattern of looping lines and spirals had been etched into the outside, continuing the patterns spread throughout the Levaanton complex. To those who knew how to read them, they told the story of her ancestors, before they had come to Talamh.

Before they'd been trapped on the planet surface by the dark workings of the Haze.

But Serena had no time for history legends this day. Her father and the other princes would already be inside. Her presence was not expected, but as her father's only child, nor could they easily preclude her.

Her gaze drifted to the slums beyond the window. To Goma. Fire still burned in the areas close to the arena. For seven days the humans had rioted. Every day since her defeat to the human.

Her father and the princes had tried to hide it of course, but not even Aiden Levaanton had the power to stay the winds of rumour. The tale had spread through the city like wildfire, until every street was abuzz with the news.

The true fires had soon followed.

Serena wondered why they did it. Why a species

capable of such wonder would burn their own homes. It certainly wasn't like the flames would harm the Alfur high in their towers. Yet each night, the humans of Goma would break their curfew and run rampant through the streets, smashing and burning, even killing their own.

Under other circumstances, she might have thought it a malfunction of their Manus readers. Every human was implanted with one of the devices before adolescence. The Manus readers suppressed their inherent Light, protecting the humans from the deleterious effects of the Haze. What was happening below was very much like what might happen had there been a mass failure of the devices.

But every diagnostic test run by the Alfurian engineers showed the devices were functioning correctly.

Which meant the humans were acting of their own volition.

Serena shivered. Her species had no body hair like humans, and the effect was more of a fully body trembling. She clenched her fist in an effort to control the reaction. It would do no good to appear so disturbed before her father and the other princes.

The streets below were mostly quiet this morning, absent of the usual bustle of daylight hours. She wondered why the humans left it to the night to do their damage, rather than daylight. With Light itself burning in their veins, the Alfur could see perfectly fine in the night. Perhaps it was just a leftover instinct, a remnant of the beasts from which humanity had evolved...

Serena shook herself.

She couldn't fall into that mindset. Of looking upon humanity as simple animals. It was an easy trap, living as they did so high above their subjects. Those few humans she glimpsed below appeared as ants beyond the glass. No wonder so many of her people had come to view them as inconsequential, insects to be squashed beneath Alfurian boots.

That needed to change.

The doors hissed open as Serena stepped towards them, detecting her personal signature in the Manus reader implanted in her palm. It appeared like those of the humans, a metallic cylinder with an orb of crystal in its centre.

The similarities ended there. Where those of the humans was designed to sypher away Light, hers allowed her to channel the energy that pulsed in her veins. It granted her incredible abilities, the power to move like death itself, or to heal, whichever she chose.

Silence fell within the council chambers as she entered. A dozen pale faces turned to watch her approach. The five princes of Talamh sat in their gilded thrones around a circular table. No other heirs were present, but that was not unexpected. While technically invited, the heirs held no power in these chambers.

Serena was no exception, but she liked to show up on occasion anyway.

A tension hung in the air as she approached the princes' table. She held her head high, eyes unbowed before the Alfur who controlled the fate of every being upon Talamh.

Of the five, one watched her with outright hostility. Darryl Sandoval, prince of the dessert city of Riesor was no friend of humanity—or Serena for that matter. He'd made his opinion on mouthy heirs quite clear on any number of occasions. He was also a warmonger, and hated the humans beneath their cities with a passion that seemed almost personal.

"Sandoval!" she exclaimed. "I heard a rumour you'd choked on a vial of Light. I'm so glad to find your demise was mostly overstated."

A rumble of discontent slid from the eldest prince as he started to his feet. "Insolent child," he growled, "the day you—"

But Serena was already moving on to a friendlier face at the table—that of her former compatriot, prince Willis Gardiner, who had only risen to prince in recent years after the death of his father.

"Willis," she said, her warmth genuine now. "So good to see you again. How goes things in Boustor?"

"Cold," Willis replied. "Though no colder than usual, sadly. Are you sure you do not wish to trade cities?"

Serena chuckled. "Again, I must politely decline, my prince. The mountain climate does not suit me."

Willis grunted. Truth was, the harsh mountains of Boustor didn't suit any of the Alfur, but someone needed to oversee the mineral rich mines of the region.

"Daughter," her father was next around the table.

Wearing long flowing robes of emerald silk, he rose at her approach. His face remained carefully free of emotion, but she knew him too well, and could see the anger behind his eyes. Those eyes, a golden yellow rather than the usual Alfurian silver, were the symbol of their royalty—and their power. All those around the table possessed the same golden hue.

"You are late," her father continued after a moment's pause. "This is most improper—"

"Improper, Father?" she asked, coming to a stop beside his place at the table and adopting her voice to his haughty tone. "Why I thought it improper that you neglected to send my invitation to this meeting."

"We thought it wise to allow you to rest after your injuries," her father replied, the slightest of frowns creasing his brow.

"I see," she mused, "and yet, you didn't think it might be wise to include me in your discussion on how to punish the one who gave me those injuries?

"That is *not* what we are here to discuss."

"Oh?"

There was an awkward pause, and Serena allowed herself the slightest of smiles. A smaller chair stood alongside her father's throne, as one did beside each of the princes, but Serena made no move to take her seat. She allowed her eyes to roam around the circular table instead.

"Pray, tell me then, what are we here to discuss?" she asked lightly.

"The riots in your damned city, of course," Sandoval

snapped. "Riots, I'll remind you, that *I* predicted would be the result of your antics in the arena."

"Did you?" Serena asked sweetly, fluttering her eyes in a distinctly human manner. "I don't recall...*oh!* Yes, I do remember something of the sort. Were not your exact words 'riots before the year is out'?" She looked around the table, eyes lifted in question. "Does anyone know if a prediction still counts when its fifty years out of date?"

An audible growl came from the chest of Sandoval, but Willis interrupted before the Alfur could scold Serena further:

"Alfur, Alfur," he said lightly, raising his hands in a gesture of peace.

He was lightly built beneath his black robes, and practically scrawny beside the bulk of the Riesoran prince, but Serena had always appreciated his calm words. Even when what was needed was action.

"Come now," he continued, "let us show some decorum. Are we not Alfur? Serena, enough with your needling."

Serena gave an overly dramatic sigh. "Very well, Willis, you win." She sank into her tiny chair, though not before she flashed her friend a grin.

"Seven days the humans have rioted." A quiet voice spoke from the back. Konad Hassan, Prince of the island city of Mayenken and eldest of the council—of all the Alfur on Talamh, in fact. Such was his age, dark patches had formed on his skin where the Light no longer circulated, giving him a rather mottled look for an Alfur.

"Seven days. I recall the last time they rose for such a time."

"Exactly!" Darryl Sandoval exclaimed. "Not since the Arrival have we faced such a threat to our people. And all because this...this *girl* decided to play with fire."

"I beg to disagree." Serena bristled. "The humans resist because you refuse to treat them as equals."

"They are beasts, scrounging in the mud for the dregs of our civilisation," the hulking Riesoran prince said dismissively. "How can the noble eagle align itself with the rats that are its super?"

"Perhaps when the rats threaten the eagle's nest," Malachy Zavala spoke up.

Serena was surprised to find him speaking on her behalf. She and the Lutryden Prince rarely saw eye to eye —he certainly hadn't been in support of her venture into the gladiatorial arena. Though none of the council had supported *that* particular venture—not even Willis.

But then, that was why she'd done it, wasn't it? To open their eyes. To show these old Alfur they were no better than the humans. They might sit here in their gilded towers and pretend they were noble, far above the creatures crawling in the mud below. But the truth was their people were capable of just as much blood violence.

Afterall, the weapons of humanity paled in comparison to those the Alfur had created. What was a sword compared to a Manus reader? A spear to the shock sticks they armed their Enforcers with? A bow, beside the airships and their destructive blasters.

No, the council might pretend, but she knew the truth.

Serena had felt it in the arena, in the rush of Light, the pounding of her hearts.

She might have become Rotin to spite her father.

But to her great shame, she had continued because she'd enjoyed it.

"The greatest threat since the Arrival?" Willis spoke up for her, his voice incredulous. "Surely you gest, Sandoval. Back then the humans had access to their Light, and were in the full grips of the Haze. These...disturbances are trivial, surely..."

"No great gathering of humans may be considered trivial," Hassan said quietly.

"By the stars, Gardiner" Sandoval growled. "I mourn the day your father passed from our ranks. At least he understood true threat posed by humanity."

"I think we have all had a fair glimpse of that threat," Zavala chuckled. "Thanks to the antics of our dear Serena. That was quite the performance, I must admit. I really thought the human would kill you."

Serena winced at the reminder. Truth be told, so had she. The fury of the Haze had burned in the human's eyes as he'd stood over her. But only for a moment. Then, inexplicably, it had retreated. Enough that he'd regained control. For how long, no one knew. It wasn't even supposed to be possible. Better for everyone that her father had exiled him far from the city.

Better for the Alfur, at least...

"That mess in the arena is exactly why—"

"Yes, yes, my daughter should have never been there," her Father interrupted yet more rambling from Sandoval. "It is done. Now we must decide on a resolution to end the violence in our cities."

Serena blinked. "Cities?"

"Yes," Willis said, somewhat guiltily. "It would appear the rumours of your...encounter, have somehow spread."

"The merchants," Malachy Zavala surmised. He pursed his lips in disapproval "There is no such thing is a hard border with their species. Their words spread almost as quickly as their offspring."

"We must finally take a firm hand," Sandoval snapped.

Tempers were fraying, despite her father's best efforts. Serena laughed to add fuel to the fire.

"Is that not what you have tried these past five hundred years?" she asked. "Pray tell, how much further into the mud would you press the poor humans?"

"A cull."

Silence fell around the table as the eldest Alfur spoke. The lighter patches of Hassan's face dimmed with his words, as though the Light had been drained by the weight of his words. He looked around the table, meeting each of their eyes.

"Zavala and Sandoval are right," he continued at last. "The human population has grown too large for Talamh to sustain. Numbers must be culled, to prevent their own destruction—and ours."

Serena's hearts stilled. She could not have heard the old Alfur correctly. There hadn't been a cull since...well, never in her short hundred years of life. Surely what he said was in jest. Yet as Serena looked around the table, she saw Sandoval nodding his enthusiastic approval and Zavala looking thoughtful. Only her father and Willis had not leapt on the idea—

"The suggestion has merits," her father announced.

"*What?*"

It was too much. Suddenly her hearts were no longer silent, but racing. Light spilled from her flesh as she came to her feet, her inner glow lighting up the room. Of the princes, only Sandoval met her eyes—and he wore a triumphant grin.

"Surely there must be another way," Willis said weakly.

"No," the old Alfur's words were like iron. "The Haze is gathering force. Our monitoring shows as much. It is attracted to their festering cities like plague rats to a corpse. Left unchecked...Aiden, Sandoval, Zavala. You know the results."

The other princes fell silent at Hassan's words. Willis slumped in his seat. The young prince knew when the tide had turned against him. But Serena had no such good sense.

"You cannot be serious?" She breathed, trying and failing to maintain her calm. "If you do this, there will never be an accord with the humans. They will hate us until the last child perishes from this planet."

"Let them hate," Sandoval sneered. "The eagle does not care for the rat's feelings."

"It is only logical," Zavala added, his voice calm, detached of emotion.

"We do not contemplate these acts out of anger or hatred, child," the eldest agreed. "Only cold logic. Left to continue this path, the humans would succumb to the Haze and destroy themselves. We only act now to spare a greater suffering later."

"Bullshit," Serena snapped, drawing gasps from around the world. "Logic? No, You act from fear. I can see it in your eyes. You know the power the humans possess, and seek only to save yourselves."

"Daughter!" Her father bellowed, coming to his feet. "Cease your impudence—"

"*My* impudence?" she snorted. "You're the ones talking of genocide."

"The humans reap only the outcome of your own actions, Serena Levaanton," Sandoval snarled, standing as well. "If blame must fall for this atrocity, let it sit on the shoulders of Rotin, who so stirred the rages of our subjects."

Serena stared at the Alfur for a long moment, her skin burning, chest rising and falling with each angry breath.

"Very well," she said at last, her voice tightly controlled, least she launch herself across the table at the Alfur. "Believe your own lies if you will. But I will partake no more in discussions of genocide. But I bid you remember. The human I fought in the arena lives. If he learns of your plan, I doubt you would survive his anger."

"Rydian Holt is far from here," her father answers,

golden eyes flashing with his own rage. "And will have succumbed days ago to the Haze, without a Manus reader."

"You had better pray to the stars it is so, Father," Serena whispered.

ONE

Fire.

That was the Haze. A burning, searing presence at the rear of Rydian's mind. No, not just the rear. All of him. It surrounded his consciousness, a constant pressure that grew each time he used the Light. A great, burning hand that was closing ever so slowly about his fragile consciousness.

Jungle closed him in on all sides. Trees dense with ferns and vines. Humid air he struggled to breathe. Such heat, the sweat never left him, not even in the dark of night.

How long now had he wandered? Days? Weeks? Time had no meaning now, not with the Haze. Not with the agony of its fiery touch. Not with the Light within.

Nor for his grief.

But that was a different sort of pain. A raw, almost physical agony, compared to the Haze. At times, the sharp reality of his father's death was the only thing Rydian had left to cling to, his anchor in reality, the tether that held him to the world, to a reality where he had loved, and lost.

Still each day, it grew a little less. Another fragment burned in the Haze. And Rydian's hold on reality grew ever fainter.

Worse still, when he was forced to use the Light. That became his measure of time, better than the passage between day and night. What did he care for passage of the sun in the sky, when it was the Light that gave him glory, that brought him to agony, that saw him take each step towards the precipice of madness?

He had tried not to use it, of course. After he'd almost lost himself that first time in Goma, Rydian had tried to lock the power away, to bury it deep. But the jungle would not relent. Day and night the creatures came for him. Without sword or shield or armour, he had only one defence.

So when the hounds came in their packs, and the primates with their howling, and greater beasts still, Rydian met them with the Light. With exhilaration, and bloodlust, and ecstasy.

And pain.

And each time the creatures fell back, he found himself lessened, his mind carved up with chunks missing, disappeared into the void of his madness.

Ten times now he had used the power. Ten moments of weakness—and power. That was how long he had wandered mindlessly in this jungle.

Now he could feel the precipice before him, the sweet release of madness beckoning. He feared his mind would not survive another burst of Light.

Rydian shivered, cold despite the crackling of his campfire. The darkness pressed against its flickering glow. He found it comforting even now, that orange light. His mind might now know the Light was a part of him, but to Rydian, that mystical force would always be associated with the Alfur, and their control over humanity.

Still, beyond the Haze and the pain, there was a part of Rydian that had embraced his connection with the Light. That accepted this was his natural state. Without even touching the burning in his core, his senses were expanded, giving him an added sense of the world around him. Or perhaps not added—rather, a sense long denied him by the Alfur.

Life was all around. Creatures big and small, each like Rydian born of the Light—and suffering for it.

That made him wonder. How had life on Talamh come to find such a balance. To adapt with such a power as the Haze, that drove all life on the planet insane?

Well, all life but the Alfur.

The question rose in his mind, then slipped back beneath the surface. He closed his eyes, exhaustion—both physical and mental—weighing heavy on his shoulders. The warmth of the fire bathed his face, bringing some small measure of peace. At least he did not have to worry for its fuel. After a lifetime of hoarding lamp oil, the stakes of wood beneath the trees was a rare joy amidst the gloom of the jungle.

But joy would not save Rydian from the madness.

And wandering aimlessly through the jungle would not free his people from the Alfur.

He sighed and took a stick to prod the fire. It crackled as he fed more fuel to the hungry tongues of flame. There was a piece of him that he'd unleashed his Light upon the Alfur in Goma, and to hell with the consequences. At the very least, he could have caused untold destruction amongst their alien overlords.

But that would have only doomed his people in the end. Doomed them to the same pain Rydian now suffered. To the lashes of the Haze, to a slow, creeping madness, the crumbling of their sanity, of civilisation itself...

...at least, if Aiden Levaanton was to be believed.

The Alfurian prince had seemed a straightforward kind of creature, but Rydian could not bring himself to altogether believe his words.

Or maybe it was just that he didn't want too.

Because believing the prince meant Rydian must accept the story about his people. That humanity before the Alfur had been little more than animals. That it had been the Alfur who had freed them from the Haze, given them sentience. That humanity owed everything to their alien overlords.

Rydian clenched his fists, allowing the glow of his artificial hand to brighten the shadows beneath the nearby trees. That was what the Alfur had given him. A life of slavery. Of bondage. A part of him chained against his will, only freed when their champion had cut off his hand.

He owed them nothing.

He could not act against the Alfur until he learned more of their past and the dangers of the Haze.

But nor would he simply rest. Rydian would not surrender to the madness until he had done all he could to free his people. That was why they'd sent him here, of course. To prevent his interference. The prince was not so foolish as to risk a battle in the middle of his city.

He scrunched his eyes closed as the pounding in his skull intensified. If only he'd still had his own Manus reader, he might reactivate it—if only for a time. No doubt that had been another of the prince's calculations. Send Rydian far away, with no access to a Manus reader to protect his mind, and let the Haze do the Alfurs' work for them.

Rydian should have seen it, but even then his mind had been made sluggish by the pain, by the pounding of the Haze against his consciousness. At times it felt as though his mind were swimming through the gelatine they gave out at times at the meat works. Even simple tasks like lighting the fire were becoming difficult now. And all the while, a voice whispered for him to use the Light...

Crack.

Rydian's head jerked at the sound of a branch breaking. His heart suddenly racing, he came to his feet. The glow of his right hand brightened further, casting back the shadows.

A pair of yellow eyes stared back at him.

A shiver ran down his spine. Those were not the eyes of a hound, or primate, or any other creature he had faced in the long days of misery. This was a creature whispered of around the fires of alleyways back in Goma.

King in its domain, the great cat watched him from the shadows, black spots on orange fur blending with the darkness. Muscles rippled as the beast realised it had been seen. But rather than retreat, it advanced into the firelight. A growl rumbled from the depths of its throat and teeth the size of daggers glinted in the dark.

Rydian shivered at the thought of those teeth closing about his throat, of his blood pouring forth, of the darkness rising to swallow him up...

...and somehow found his soul growing peaceful. After so many days of pain, suffering the fiery lashes of the Haze, the darkness, emptiness...it seemed almost inviting. To finally escape the agony, to be at peace—

Rydian's eyes were just drooping closed when something within him reacted. Light burst to life within, casting back his weary acceptance, his yearning for the darkness. Rage replaced it. Realisation struck Rydian like a bolt of condensed energy. Not only was this beast a king, it too possessed Light, had used some dark aspect of its power to set its prey at ease.

But not Rydian. This creature was not the only one born to the Light.

"Nice try," he growled, a blade of burning Light appearing in his hand.

For just a second, he savoured the rush of power he experienced, the knowledge *he* was king in this place, that the world bowed at his feet. For a second, the Light banished the pain, the voices, the screaming, and Rydian was himself again. The youth from the slums of Goma. Son of Jasmine and Rafael. Gladiator. Warrior. Human.

Then, like a dam bursting in his mind, the Haze tore through the cracks in his mind, and the pain returned. He should have fallen to his knees as the first screams washed over him, should have collapsed from that infinitum of collective pain—if not for one thing.

Rage.

A roar came from the great cat as they came together, claw and Light blade seeking blood. Rydian was fast, his Light fuelled muscles propelling him across the soft Talamh of the jungle in a single bound.

The cat was faster still.

Powerful muscles sent the cat hurtling for Rydian, and only a last minute twist of his torso kept it from tearing out his throat. The air hummed as burning Light of his blade cut empty space.

Pain tore down Rydian's side.

He gasped and leapt back from the beast. A curse slipped from his lips. His hand fell to his side and he felt the welts the claws had left. Blood streaked his fingers when he lifted them to the light. He felt a momentary panic. Rydian hadn't faced a threat like this before, not another creature of the Light.

Of the Haze.

He could see the burning behind the great cat's eyes now, could sense its anger. It stalked towards him, power radiating through its being, madness in its mind.

Human and great cat came together again, tooth and claw meeting Light. The eddies of the Haze swelled as they did battle, the pressure upon Rydian's mind increasing with each clash. The pain came with it, a thousand needles stabbing into his skull, until he felt his sanity approaching the precipice.

Rydian screamed. Not from talons or tooth, but the burning of his mind. The end approached, but he would not be destroyed, would not surrender to the madness of his foe. He stumbled, somehow evading the beast's terrible jaws. A voice within screamed to be unleased, but Rydian resisted. Just. He could not become like this creature, driven mad by the Haze, living only for destruction for his next meal. There were those that needed him...

He alighted in the shadow of a tree, and paused, blade raised in preparation for another strike.

The creature stalked through the shadows, eyes aglow, but now Rydian found himself wondering. What had this creature been before the Haze had taken hold? Before it had reached adolescence and the Light within had woken. If humans, for all their power in the Light, possessed a consciousness before the Haze, what of this creature?

The Alfur had freed humanity of the Haze. But that did not mean they were the only species on Talamh with the possibility of sentience...

A memory came back to Rydian, of the old hound that

Marcus Aureli, had kept by his side. The beast should have been mad, driven insane by the Haze. Instead, it had followed his mentor around like a tame puppy. Somehow, Aureli had freed the creature from the madness that afflicted every other mammal on Talamh.

Could Rydian do the same?

He shivered. The leopard had paused as well. The great globes of its eyes watched him. The Haze shown within, burning with frustration, that it had not managed to destroy this foe. He felt that same fury, the burning need to destroy this challenger, to prove himself superior—

Rydian shook himself. That was not him. He had no need to prove his skill by killing. Only to survive. And perhaps, on this occasion, there was another way.

Light bloomed at his fingertips. Not the burning Light of battle, but a softer kind. The kind the Alfur summoned when they used their Manus readers for healing, rather than destruction.

A rumble came from the leopard. Before it had met his violence with violence of its own. Now it retreated a step. Sensing its confusion, Rydian stepped towards it. A shared pain hung between them, that burning, tangible part of the Haze that reached out and flayed them with its fiery whips. No creature, human, beast, or otherwise, could withstand that torture. Not forever.

The great cat had ceased to back away now. It watched him come, body taut, muscles prepared to spring. Rydian was not deterred. He knew to fight on would mean his destruction. Even if he defeated this creature, the Haze would sweep him away eventually. So why not try something else? Some desperate gamble?

When Rydian rested his hand on the enormous head of the beast, he half-expected the creature to turn and tear it from his arm. But the cat did not move. For a moment, they stood terse, man and beast locked now in silent battle. Light pulsed within each, twin fires in the darkness.

Then as though a dam were bursting, the twin fires combined, Light swirling between the two, joining, uniting in a burst of white.

A shudder went through man and beast as they found themselves absent of pain.

Silence fell.

And into the silence, a voice.

Greetings, Light Giver.

TWO

A BLADE FLASHED FOR HAZEL'S FACE. EVEN BLUNTED, it would sting—if not outright break bones—if she let it land. She spun away instead, laughing harshly as her opponent staggered. Thrown off-balance by the power he'd put behind his swing, he stumbled several steps before righting himself. A kick hard in the back from Hazel put an end to that.

He fell hard, slamming face-first into the sands of the training ground.

Still laughing, Hazel turned to the ring of Goman gladiators.

"Well?" she asked raising shield and sword in an invitation. "Who's next?"

Her next opponent was one of the freshly landed recruits. He didn't even have a name yet, let alone a chosen weapon. He came at Hazel with gladius in hand, face pale as he raised the shield before him. The expression on his face suggested he would rather be anywhere else than facing the woman before him.

Hazel tisked. His fear was so great, he'd already forgotten her instruction for the shield. He held it too high, cringing beneath the iron trim, as though that alone would save him.

No matter. Hazel had a technique for correcting bad habits.

A cry rang through the training complex as she hammered her sword into the shield, wrenching it sideways in the man's grip. To the recruit's credit, he tried a clumsy stab as she raised her sword again, forcing her to skip back a foot. But it was only a delaying tactic. A second strike from her sword wrenched the shield from the recruit's grip.

He stood there a moment, mouth open, exposed.

Hazel completed his lesson by ramming the rim of her own shield into his ribs. Caught off-guard, the wind hissed between the recruit's teeth. The red colour of his cheeks drained away as, wheezing, he staggered back from Hazel. But there was no escaping her words.

"Your shield is as much a weapon as your sword." Her voice rang from the stone walls.

She leapt forward again as the recruit straightened. This time she put all her weight behind the blow. There was a sickening *crack* as her shield struck her foe in the face.

The impact flung him to the ground where his predecessor was still shaking off their own beating.

Satisfied the lesson had been learnt, Hazel turned to the remaining gladiators for another sparring partner. At that moment, a bell sounded, signalling the end of the hour. Their time in the practice ring was at an end. If she remembered the schedule correctly the Riesoran gladiators had the next hour.

The crunch of sand beneath heavy boots alerted her to Johanas's approach. A smile touched her face as she turned and nodded a greeting to the new Goman weapons master. He loomed over her, easily twice her size, his muscles still well-honed from their time training beneath Marcus Aureli. He handed her a water skin. She drank greedily.

"You sure you don't want back in?" she asked when she'd finished.

Johanas looked from her to the recruit, who had only just regained his breath. "Even if the Alfur would permit me to return, you know how I feel about violence, Hazel."

She frowned at his use of her real name around the other gladiators, but he was already moving towards the young recruit. She watched as he offered the young man a hand, then passed him another water skin. The Alfur had forbidden Johanas from so much as stepping foot in one of the four cities again, after his actions the month prior, when he'd raised the ire of their home crowd by refusing to fight. That in itself was no small penalty—Johanas's father was still in Goma, and the sentence meant he would never see the man again.

But after what she had witnessed of Alfurian mercy,

Hazel could not understand how it hadn't been worse. Her brother and the other rebels had been executed on the spot —and they had only broken into a forbidden building. Johanas had raised a stadium of humans to riot. It was a wonder they hadn't put him down on the spot.

Still, she would not look this particular gift-horse in the mouth. She had lost enough friends and loved ones.

"Draw in a big breath, there you go. That hurts? Where?" Johanas was saying to the recruit. He flashed a glare over his shoulder as Hazel joined them. Hazel tried to recall the young man's name, and failed. Too many had passed through the camp over the last few months. No wonder Falcon and Aureli didn't bother to learn names until a recruit had survived their first bout.

"I think you might have fractured a rib," Johanas announced after several prods at the recruit's chest. "Go see Falcon. She'll ensure you're in line for a healing before your first bout. You'll have to take it easy with training until the next games though."

The man moved away, though not without a glare in Hazel's direction. She offered him a smile that said he was welcome to a rematch whenever he wanted. The last of his colour drained away at that and he scampered away without another word. She laughed deep in her throat.

"Taking your anger out on the recruits isn't going to help anyone."

Hazel's smile slipped away at Johanas's words. They cast a shadow across the excitement of the afternoon's festivities.

"I'm just preparing them for reality," she said, her tone harsher than she'd intended. "You know better than anyone they'll find no mercy in the arena. Better they break a few bones here, than die out there."

"That is not how we were trained."

"And look where that got us," Hazel snapped.

Johana said nothing for a long moment. "You are not angry with me, Hazel. Or the recruits, for that matter."

The breath hissed between Hazel's teeth as she exhaled and looked. Suddenly, she could not bare to meet her friend's pale green eyes. He was right, of course. Even now, weeks later, that moment in the arena kept playing through her thoughts, whenever her mind was unoccupied. Rydian lying prone before her. Her blade poised to strike. The anger bubbling in her veins, screaming for Hazel to claim her revenge...

...and the old man stumbling across the sands, placing himself between her blade and Rydian.

The scream as he died.

"When will you stop blaming yourself?" Johanas's voice was quiet now, inaudible to the other recruits still filing from the training square.

"I don't blame myself!" Hazel snarled.

She swung on him, practice blade raised, but Johanas did not retreat like the other gladiators. There was no sign of fear in his eyes as he stared her down.

"I blame Rydian," she ground out, the words almost catching in her throat. "It was him I wanted to kill."

"He was our friend."

"Only because he lied to us! Because he tricked us!"

"Rydian was not responsible for your brother's death." Still the giant's emerald eyes watched her. There was no violence in those eyes, no anger or judgement. Only...Johanas. He wasn't like her. Wasn't like Rydian or Falcon or any of the others in this awful place. There was not a violent bone in his body. How the Alfur could have ever considered him a threat was beyond Hazel.

She swallowed a lump lodged in her throat. "No, but his mother was," she croaked. "Wherever she is, alive or dead, I want her to suffer. To know the loss I felt."

Johanas laid a hand on her shoulder. "You would kill an innocent man, your own friend, for the crimes of his mother?"

Hazel lowered her head but said nothing. It sounded worse, coming from the peaceful giant. Bad enough that she would not say her answer outload. But the truth sounded like a bell within her.

Yes, I would.

"If you would go that far," Johanas continued as though he'd heard her unspoken words. "Then how are you any better than the Alfur?"

"*What?*" Hazel's head snapped up. "How dare—"

"How dare I?" Johanas's voice never rose an octave, but its rumble stopped Hazel in her tracks. "How dare *you*, Hazel?" he whispered. "Rydian is my friend, just as much as you. We both know I would be dead on those sands if not for him."

"We both came for you…" Hazel started to say, but the words died on her tongue as she looked into Johanas's eyes.

His hand tightened on her shoulder. "I know you're angry," he said softly. He released her. "You have every right to be. But none of this is your fault. Neither is it Rydian's. We're all just pawns in a greater game."

The sound of voices carried from the corridor. They looked around as the door to the practice ground opened. The last of their teammates had already left the sands, and now they stood alone as the Riesorans arrived. The red-garbed gladiators paused as they noticed the two Gomans.

"My, my, what have we here?" It was Samiyah, the Riesoran champion. "Two Goman rejects." She laughed. "I wonder if they'll ever let us fight in Goma again. You folks royally screwed yourselves, didn't you? Particularly you, big man."

Hazel bristled, but Johanas's hand on her shoulder kept her from doing anything rash. The woman's words cut deep. While the Alfur had nothing official to say on the subject, there hadn't been a games hosted in Goma since the incident—and it didn't appear likely they would have a home bout anytime soon.

"Honestly, I'm surprised Falcon didn't put you both out on your asses with your friend, Mouse."

This time the woman's words were too much. Growling, Hazel tried to shrug of Johanas's hand and reach for her practice blade, but the giant weapon's master held her still. Laughter came from the Riesorans as they turned their backs, dismissing her without another glance.

"They're not the enemy either," Johanas said softly.

Hazel let out a long exhalation, but finally she nodded and allowed Johanas to lead her from the grounds. The ringing of laughter chased after them. Hazel grated her teeth. They might not be her true enemy, but at least she would have a chance to make them pay. Sooner or later, she would face them in the arena.

Then they would see who was left laughing.

THREE

PEACE.

Rydian could hardly believe it. For the first time in weeks, the voices had fallen silent. The screams had become a distant whisper. Claws no longer racked his mind, no longer sank their tender hooks in his consciousness.

He existed now in a fragile state of equilibrium. A bond had formed between himself and the great cat in that moment of madness. Now it provided a shelter for both amidst the raging storm that was the Haze.

How it had come into being, or how long it would last, Rydian couldn't say. All he could feel in this moment was relief. Relief that the torture he had suffered had eased, that he no longer stood at the precipice of madness.

He sensed similar emotions from the great cat. It was a leopard, he remembered now that the Haze no longer burned him. King of the jungle. There hadn't been a sighting of one in Goma in a generation. It had not spoken again since that first moment of bonding, but he could still sense its intelligence through their bond. And its relief. For if Rydian had suffered these past weeks, he could only imagine the agony of an entire life spent under the weight of the Haze.

Not that that fate was entirely off the table. Beyond the shelter of their bond, he could sense the Haze still. It had not vanished. It lingered at the edges of his mind, a dark presence, a promise that one day it would find a way to return, to claim him once again. One day, it would claim them all.

But not this day.

Wandering through the jungle, Rydian found himself whistling an old song from his childhood. It was a tune his mother had taught him, he thought, though the memories were faint. He couldn't recall the words, but it had been a jingling tune about the perils of Talamh. Something about dogs hounding the city walls and felines prowling the shadows.

A snort came from his side as he imagined hordes of furry felines hunting a human in the alleys of Goma. A sense of mirth came across the link with the leopard at the thought of fleeing its tiny cousins.

"You never had a dozen of them chasing you," Rydian said without breaking stride. "You swipe one away...and the others slip beneath your guard. So many tiny teeth and claws..." He shuddered, the tune dying on his lips as he glimpsed at the shadows of a nearby tree.

They were walking with no particular destination—having no particular place to be. Just enjoying their newfound peace. Now that his mind was clear, Rydian knew he'd been far more gone than he'd realised. To his mind, he'd been staving off the madness, but he could see clearly now. He'd been little better than the leopard by the time they'd connected.

It was galling in a way. To know he possessed such power, yet to be so controlled by it. Within him, and every human, was the power they'd always needed to set themselves free, to drive the Alfur from their planet. But so long as the Alfur controlled the secrets of the Manus readers, doing so would only consign his people to madness. The same madness that had consumed their ancestors...

Rydian shivered, clenching his Light-hand. He wouldn't allow that to happen. Better a life of slavery than to have everything about his people consumed by the Haze.

But Rydian would not settle for either. He clung to the words of Rotin, before he'd stepped onto the ship and into exile. She'd promised him there was more. About his mother. About the Alfur, and the Haze. He sensed she did not know it all herself, but so long as secrets remained, there was also hope.

That hope centred around whatever his mother had uncovered in the Alfurian temple. Though that in itself was not without risks. He no longer denied the truth about his mother. He had seen it in his friends eyes, that day on the sands of the arena. His mother had killed Hazel's brother, had turned against the resistance.

But Rydian suspected it had not been at her own will.

Something within the Alfurian temple had corrupted his mother. Released her Light, perhaps, exposing her to the Haze. It was the only thing that made sense to Rydian. Nothing else could have made his mother turn against her own kind.

A rumble came from Rydian's side. He forced his attention back to the present. They were still trapped in the middle of the Talamh jungle. His new companion had spared him the ravaging of the Haze, given him peace and a second set of eyes. But they were far from safe. Even two Light imbued beings could not be entirely secure in the wilds.

And peace did not come without its own disadvantages. Now Rydian was no longer overwhelmed by his inner pain, he found more than enough discomforts to occupy his thoughts. The heat was stifling, and sweat ran constantly down his face, stinging as it dripped into his eyes. The buzzing of mosquitos was near continuous, their bites coming day and night to sate their merciless blood-lust. The itching he woke to each morning was far worse than anything he'd experienced, even in the monsoon season of Goma.

Soon Rydian found himself longing for the sparse luxuries of the gladiator complex. That had been in the middle of the jungle too, but at least there a breeze had often blown across the open field, tasting of salt and the unknown ocean.

Well, unknown until that awful night with Aureli. Even now, the memory of that night was equal part glory, and grief. Standing on that sandy shore, tasting the salty air, listening to the crashing of the waves against the shore, he could almost think himself free.

But Aureli's death had brought all those hopes crashing back to Talamh.

Another rumble came from his side, and the beast spoke. *This...Aureli...was a Light Giver?*

"No," Rydian said, then frowned. What if Aureli *had* been a Light Giver? He'd warned Rydian about the Haze, after all. Or at least, he'd said something along those lines. And there had been the hound the man had kept, just as Rydian now had the leopard. He cursed beneath his breath. "Maybe."

Perhaps this Aureli knows more of our plight.

"He's gone," Rydian replied, then paused, thinking of his conversations with Falcon. "Though...his knowledge might survive. He had an apprentice."

We should speak with her.

Rydian snorted. "We should. But for all I know, she could be on the other side of the planet. I have no idea where we are—or where the gladiator complex is." He sighed. "A shame I don't have a Manus reader. I could probably pull up a map of Talamh and figure out where we were in relation to the complex. See if it would even be possible to walk there."

Silence hung between man and beast for a time. They continued through the trees, following a stream, leaping from one moss covered rock to the next. The waters were clouded and Rydian kept well back from the edge. Who knew what might lurk beneath that murky surface?

This device, the great cat's words came as the trees opened up a little, gifting Rydian a glorious moment in the emerald sun. *It was powered by your Light.*

"More like it suppressed my Light," Rydian muttered. "The Alfur use them to shield humans from the Haze. Or that's what they claim. I think they're more concerned about controlling us."

A rumble from the leopard suggested it would not mind that exchange. Rydian sensed the fear in the creature, its innate terror that the madness would return, that the Haze would claim it once more.

It would seem that if this device was suppressing your Light, the leopard mused. *Then anything you could do with your Manus reader, it would follow would still be possible.*

Rydian stopped in his tracks. "What?"

It stands to reason—

"Yeah, yeah, I got that," Rydian cut off the creature. Suddenly his heart was racing.

Surely it couldn't be that simple?

His eyes fell to his palm. The Light-hand was a perfect replica of the one he had lost. A cylindrical tube had even formed in his palm to replace the Manus reader he'd had since adolescence. He swallowed, then clenching his eyes and fist closed, Rydian concentrated as he had back when he'd lived in Goma and wanted to chart a route home.

A soft humming told him it had worked. When he opened his eyes, a great ball of Light had taken shape before them. Talamh. At first the surface seemed smooth, but before his eyes it continued to change. Oceans appeared, great spans of water dyed a darker shade that the rest of the Light. The waters of Talamh were far greater than he'd thought. They took up much of the globe, in fact.

But he didn't want the ocean just now. Rydian needed to know where *he* was. The globe began to turn slowly in place. A handful of dots marked the locations of the five cities, set at intervals around the globe. He watched the globe turn, concentrating on himself, on where he was—

There!

His companion saw it at the same time as Rydian. His heart pulsed as the blinking red dot appeared on the globe. Deep in the jungles of one of the continents. The same one as Goma—but far, far away from the city. Hundreds of miles. It would take a lifetime to cross that expanse, surely.

But Rydian *was* close to the coast. He wondered...

The globe flattened and the area in which he was located grew larger. Rydian watched, breath held, as valleys took shape, and rivers and mountains, even the individual trees and boulders. So detailed, he wondered how it could be possible. This was no projection from a map someone had drawn, but a true representation of Talamh. Right down to the smallest blade of grass.

And there, nestled just off the coast, an open area and a tiny collection of buildings. Probably the only buildings that existed on this entire planet outside the cities.

The gladiator complex.

It was still far away from his own red dot. Miles upon miles from where Rydian and the great cat stood. But Light was burning in Rydian's veins. Light he could now use without fear of madness. Light that could power him through the days and nights.

Light he could fight back with.

And maybe teach others to use.

FOUR

Serena stalked down the long corridors of the Levaanton tower, her boots tapping in an obscenely loud manner on the metallic floors. The Alfur were noble creatures, elegant, graceful—and above all, silent. They did not make loud tapping noises as they walked, but rather announced their arrival with softly spoken words and a glint of Light.

Which was why for the past weeks, Serena had chosen to wear a pair of steel-capped human boots.

Only a few dozen Alfur lived in each of their towers, so Serena's encounters with her own kind were disappointingly rare. But she enjoyed a grin when she did come upon them, as she did now. The sorry creature leaped on the spot as the tapping of her boots approached. Eyes wide in fright, he raised his Manus reader, as though he expected a human to come barrelling down upon him.

Instead, he was greeted to the sight of the Goman heir

striding towards him. The look on the Alfur's face was priceless as he realised his mistake. Suddenly he was frozen, palm still lifted, his eyes darting around the broad corridor—even looking out the great window of glass—before finally settling on Serena.

Only then did he finally dip into a bow and stammer out a greeting.

Raising her nose as though offended by his disrespect, Serena stalked passed him and continued on her way.

Just now, she had better places to be than tormenting her distant relatives. Outside, the emerald sun was setting over Goma, signalling the end of her official engagements for the day.

Which left only the one unofficial, somewhat clandestine meeting in her apartments. Clandestine not because it was a particularly great secret, but because of who she was meeting, and what they intended to discuss.

She and the other heirs had been meeting for years now to debate and discuss the governing of the planet by their fathers—and how they would do things differently when their time came. It was with the other heirs Serena had first discussed her idea of becoming Rotin. And more recently, even more far fetched ideas. Like the freedom of humanity.

The doors to Serena's chambers hissed open at her approach. The sound of voices and laughter carried into the corridor. Serena rolled her eyes. She was late, as usual, and it sounded like the others had taken the opportunity to begin without her. She'd be lucky if any of her Light was left.

"You've better have saved some for me," she announced her arrival, striding through the doors. "After the day I've had, I'm starved!"

It was true. Since retiring as Rotin, her rations of Light had been reduced drastically. Apparently a heir needed far less than a gladiator. Her injured arm was one thing—at least that was now almost healed—but the cravings she now suffered was something she struggled to ignore.

"You, starved?" Cassia Sandoval exclaimed. The daughter of the Riesoran prince was his opposite in every way—and one of Serena's closest friends. Perhaps that was why Cassia's father loathed her so much, thinking her wayward habits had rubbed off on his daughter. "Honestly Serena," the heir of Riesor continued. "We can see the Light shining through your skin, remember? You could go a week without eating with what you've already got and still be brighter than me!"

"Hardly," Serena muttered, before stepping forward and embracing her friend in a most un-Alfurian way.

Cassia grinned as they drew apart. She held Serena by the shoulders for a moment, as though to inspect her. "Alright, maybe not a week," she conceded.

Serena snorted. "Thanks," she said wryly.

An audible rumble came from her stomach. Chuckling, her friend stood to the side, allowing Serena access to the jug of Light on the table. The others murmured greetings and she poured herself a glass, before turning to the others.

The three heirs sat around her round table—a smaller, less official version of the council's. Nate Hassan was quiet like his elderly father, though not nearly so conservative when it came to humans. His father might be eldest of the Alfur, but he was youngest of the heirs—something for which he had yet to hear the end of.

Their last member was Yisroel Zavala, heir to Lutryde and probably the least sympathetic to the human cause. She had joined their meetings reluctantly in the beginning, and while Serena thought they'd made some practice with her, she was also sure the Lutryden heir was quick to pass on all that was said in these meetings to her father. That didn't overly bother Serena—she'd hoped their discussion might bring about a softening in Yisroel. Alas, that gamble did not appear to have paid off.

"They've got the rest of us on rations, you know," Nate offered as Serena took her seat at the table. "Ever since your little stunt with the human."

"I'd hardly call it a stunt," Serena said, pursing her lips. "He could have killed me."

"Exactly!" Cassia exclaimed. "You cannot tell us that the first and only gladiator to defeat you in a human generation decided, by chance mind, to just spare your life?"

"Come on, Serena, you can tell us," Nate encouraged. "It's been a few weeks. That's what we're all here for anyway, right? To share the details of our top-secret plans?"

Serena rolled her eyes at her companion's youthful enthusiasm. Unlike the rest of them, Nate hadn't even passed his first half-century. "Sadly no secret plans here," she replied. "Honestly, I'd only seen him a couple times before we crossed blades. I had no idea..."

"No idea of what?" Yisroel spoke up for the first time. Her eyes shone with curiosity. "Father refused to tell even me the details about what happened in the arena."

"*My* father won't shut up about it," Cassia muttered, but she gestured for Serena to speak her part.

She shrugged. "I'm not sure why Malachy wouldn't share that detail with you, Yisroel. I cut off his hand."

The Alfur's eyes widened. "That seems...imprudent."

"I was going for the killing blow," Serena muttered. "I didn't expect him to put his bloody arm in the way."

"Language," Cassia said, though her eyes glittered with amusement.

Nate snorted. "Good luck with that, Serena's practically a space pirate at this point."

"You don't even know what that is."

"I read a book about them!"

"Quiet!" It was Yisroel who cut through the banter between the two. Eyes wide, she leaned forward across the table towards Serena. "So it's true? He used the Light?"

Serena nodded grimly. "It ended about as well as you might imagine."

"Did he..."

"Was he..."

"Light possessed?" Serena nodded. "Afraid so."

If her fellow heirs had been human, no doubt the colour would have drained from their faces, but as they were Alfur, the Light beneath their skin brightened, adding to the glow of her already well-lit chambers.

There were three kinds of beings connected to the Light. Those like the Alfur, who consumed Light but could not create it themselves, were considered Light Takers. Most other animals on the planet were Light possessed—meaning they could create their own Light. Only that power came at a cost. Those who created Light on this planet were also affected by the Haze and driven mad by it.

Yet humans were yet another step above the other animals of this planet. While dogs and cats and other mammals created small amounts of Light, each human generated enough energy to power an Alfurian ship. Which, indeed, they did with their Manus readers syphoning off their Light and thereby protecting them from the Haze.

A human without their Manus reader, however, was not only exposed to the ravaging of the Haze. They also had access to all the Light generated within their own bodies.

"Serena, how are you alive?" Cassia's voice took on a serious tone now.

Serena shrugged. "Like I said. The human chose to spare me."

"How is that even possible?" Nate mused. "His mind

should have been mush the second his Manus reader was removed."

"I won't pretend to understand it myself," Serena replied. "Like I said, I should be dead. It's a miracle he didn't obliterate me where I stood."

"It's a miracle he didn't obliterate the rest of the city along with you," Yisroel muttered. Serena had a feeling she was losing the young heir's support for the humans by the minute. Talk of freedom and liberation was a hard enough sell, but the idea of having *Light* possessed humans running around the planet would have the Alfur up in arms.

"Father would have stopped him," Serena replied. *Though not without losses.*

She didn't say the last part out loud. When the Alfur had first settled on Talamh, restraining the Light of the human population hadn't originally been about the gift of sentience. According to her father, it had been about controlling the threat the Haze induced humans posed to the newly arrived Alfur. They might have sought another planet, one free of the grips of the Haze, but...by then it had already been too late.

"You must have been born on a lucky star," Nate said quietly.

"Goma should be in ruins," Yisroel agreed. "How did your father dispose of this human?"

"He sent him into exile."

"*What?*" The three exclaimed in unison.

Serena raised her eyebrows. She hadn't realised her

father had kept that detail from the other princes. "In return for sparing my life. Who knew Father was so sentimental?"

"You mean that *thing* is still out there?" Yisroel gasped.

A scowl furrowed Serena's brow. "His name was Rydian Holt," she admonished. "And we're here to discuss the fate of those *things*, remember?"

Yisroel's face was flushed with Light. "I don't recall any discussions about letting Light possessed humans wander freely in our streets," she hissed. Her eyes glanced to her great set of windows, as though she feared the human might come barrelling through at any moment.

A sigh slipped from Serena's lips. "He's *not* wandering the streets. My father dumped him somewhere in the jungle, a long way from here. Besides, that was weeks ago now." She swallowed, mouth suddenly parched. "We all know what will have become of him by now." The Haze wasn't known for its mercy.

Silence stretched out at her words as the others exchanged glances. Nate finally broke it by clearing his throat.

"So. The council's edict. How are we going to respond?" he asked.

Serena smiled and nodded her thanks. The change of subject had been rather tactless, but it was welcome.

"We cannot let it happen," she said resolutely.

"Obviously," Cassia said, then paused. "Though I'm not sure there is anything we can do to prevent it, Serena. Not unless you're suggesting we hold a coop of our own."

"No." Her friend only spoke in gest, she knew, but they couldn't even begin to allow themselves down that path. She might not always agree with her father and the council, but their rule had seen the Alfur enjoy hundred years of peace on this planet.

"Then what do you suggest," Nate asked, his voice uncharacteristically solemn. Rising, he crossed to the window. Night had fallen now, but it was not dark. Below, fires burned. "Our fathers are right about one thing—this cannot continue."

"The flames will spread," Yisroel agreed. "If we do nothing, more will die than if they'd been culled in the first place."

"But our hands would be clean," Nate pointed out.

"I don't give a damn about our hands," Serena snapped. "Mine are stained in blood, but finally, *finally* we have the council's attention. We have to press them, show them another way."

"Self-governance?" Yisroel asked. They had discussed it several times before, but always she'd kept her silence on the topic. Now she snorted. Joining Nate at the window, she gestured to the flames. "You cannot in all seriousness stand there and tell me they are ready for that."

"They have spent the last month burning down their own homes," Nate mused.

"Under *our* governance," Serena pointed out archly.

Her fellow heirs fell silent at that. She joined them at the window and looked out at the flames. Sadness touched her heart. This was what she'd wanted, wasn't it? Her father and the council's attention. She had poked and prodded the humans all these years, hoping one day they would finally make a stand. Only...she had never imagined it would look like this.

"Surely we must agree that genocide *cannot* be the answer," she whispered.

"Of course, Serena," Cassia agreed, though she flashed a look at Yisroel, as though warning her to keep quiet. "It's just...we need a plan. Something that will bring our fathers to the negotiating table. As it is...we could talk all night, and still be no closer to a solution."

Silence fell over the room then as they stared out over the flickering glow of the city. It broke Serena's heart to see the destruction below, knowing she'd played a part in it. It *had* to lead to something, some breakthrough, an improvement for the creatures that begged at their feet. It couldn't end in yet more murder.

"We need to stop treating them like animals," she said softly.

"They need to stop acting like them," Yisroel retorted.

"Treat someone like an animal for five hundred years, they'll act in kind," Nate offered.

"He spared me," Serena said quietly. "Fear him, scorn him, but Rydian Holt showed more honour in that moment than our entire council. He had every right to kill me. The Haze was surely screaming for him to do it. He chose not to." She drew in a breath. "Surely if he could find it in his heart to show mercy, our people can do the same for humanity."

"Good luck getting our fathers to agree with that," Cassia muttered.

Serena nodded. Cassia was right. They could talk all night.

But in the end, the fate of humanity lay in the hands of her father and the other princes.

It was them she needed to convince.

FIVE

THE BOUSTORAN CROWD ROARED. A TRICKLE OF DUST drifted from the ceiling as a thousand boots pounded the stands of the arena. Hazel's nostrils twitched and she struggled to hold back a sneeze. The other gladiators shifted nervously in their seats, exchanging glances. Hazel ignored them.

Another games on foreign soil. By now it was clear to all the Goman team was being punished. Or perhaps it was just that the Alfur did not trust them not to pull off another stunt like Johanas's. Though given she and Rydian had both been more than happy to take their friend's place...

She shook herself. She could not think of Rydian. Not now. She needed her rage for the sands, not here in this dark chambers beneath the stadium.

Besides, Rydian was in all likelihood dead. That was the assumption across much of the gladiator camp. The last to hear from him had been Falcon, just before he'd challenged Rotin to single combat. No one survived crossing swords with the Alfurian gladiator...

...so why then had the Alfur not announced his death.

There were other whispers, of course. Rumours that claimed he'd defeated the infamous Rotin. Hazel had dismissed them out of hand. She knew Rydian. He was talented enough, sure. But she'd seen Rotin in action. Rydian hadn't stood a chance...

...so where then was the Alfurian champion?

"Hawk."

Hazel's head jerked up at the sound of her stadium name. It was a moment before she noticed Falcon standing over her.

"They're calling you."

Hazel came to her feet. No words passed between the two women as they stood eye to eye, watching one another. There had been little love lost between them since Hazel's first day at the gladiator complex. In her opinion, Falcon was a failure of a champion who had discarded her responsibilities to her team.

"Be careful out there," Falcon said, the words unexpected. "They've been matching us with the best since..." She paused. "We've lost enough good fighters recently."

Hazel furrowed her brow. "Since when do you care?"

The concern in Falcon's eyes boiled away. "Maybe I don't," she snapped, "but if we don't start putting on a better showing, the Alfur will have no more reason to keep us around. Don't think they've forgotten what your friend did."

The words hung in the air. Hazel did not address them. She stared at the woman a moment longer—then turned and strode through the chamber without another word. She felt the eyes of her comrades upon her as she approached the stairs, but Hazel ignored them. A name was projected alongside hers on the wall, but she ignored it. It didn't matter who the Alfur sent against her, what their name was.

They all died the same.

Her feet were light as she climbed the stairs. This was something she knew. Joining the arena, becoming a gladiator, none of this had been her choice. But she had made it hers. She was Hawk more than Hazel now.

Warrior, gladiator, killer.

And if Falcon wanted a show, she would give her one.

The crowd roared as Hawk stepped onto the sands. Not for her, of course. This was Boustor. The mountain city would not cheer for a Goman gladiator. Especially not after what had happened in Goma. All of Talamh knew of traitor that had fought for their team. The son who had betrayed the rebellion. Some even whispered that Rydian had sided with the Alfur and been taken to their sacred towers.

That might even be the truth, for all Hawk knew. She didn't care. If Rydian ever surfaced, she would kill him, just as she had killed every other gladiator to have come against her.

Just as she would kill the man the Boustoran crowd were cheering for now.

He stood across from her, dressed in the black leather of the mountain city, grinning at her approach. He lifted a sword in mock salute. She ignored him. Their time would come soon enough, when the Light barrier that separated them fell.

Seeing his efforts were wasted on her, Hawk's opponent turned to his adoring crowd and raised his arms. They cheered in enthusiasm as he acted out chopping her in half.

She let him have his fun. This was why most gladiators loved fighting in their own city. The exhilaration of knowing the crowd was on your side. That they would cheer your every move, hang on your every success and failure. That you were fighting for more than just yourself.

But what did Hawk care for her fellow humans? They had failed her at every step. Let the fools cheer, or hoot and jeer. It mattered not. She didn't fight now for Goma or Boustor or any of the five cities.

Hawk fought for herself.

Her foe finished up his work on the crowd as the drums began to sound and turned back to Hawk.

"Are you ready to taste the blade of Battleboar?" he sneered to her.

Hawk raised an eyebrow. "That's your name?" she snorted. "Very colourful."

A rumble came from the man's throat, but the drums

were growing louder now, and whatever else he had to say was drowned out by their pounding.

Hawk rolled her shoulders, loosening her joints in the final moments before the battle. The drums reached and thundering crescendo—then abruptly fell silent.

The Light-barrier blinked out.

And Battleboar attacked.

He came at her in a rush of fury, a roar on his lips, the greatsword he wielded raised high above his head. It was a terrible weapon, large enough to cut someone as small as Hawk in two with a single swing. Her shield would do nothing against the power behind its strikes—at least if she tried to meet them head on.

Hawk had no intention of doing any such thing. Thankfully, the greatsword was also an unwieldy choice of weapon. It was a simple matter for her to skip backwards out of the path of Battleboar's first swing. Her evasion only seemed to add to his fury though. Snarling, he chased after her, apparently unperturbed by her evasion.

Hawk let him come, skipping backwards and to the side, her sandaled feet moving easily in the golden sands. Her heart raced despite her calm exterior, adrenaline flooding her veins. In truth, it was a relief to be back in the arena, away from the slow toil of the gladiator complex.

The sands were all that was left to her now. The Alfur, Rydian, his mother, they had taken everything else from her. She didn't know how Johanas could bear to stay, to pass each day the same as the last, trapped in that nowhere outpost, without even the rush of battle to break the monotony.

Blood thrummed in Hawk's ears as she evaded another blow. The enormous blade rang as it slammed into the ground, sending sand showering across their feet. Her heart raced at the thrill of escaping yet again. She made no move to riposte. Couldn't risk it, with that terrible blade. Better to wait, to allow Battleboar to wear himself down, before she made her move.

The Boustoran gladiator was more than happy to oblige. He continued his assault, fury etched across hi face. Clearly, he'd taken her dismissal of his name to heart. Hawk couldn't help herself.

She began to laugh.

What else was there for her to do? It was a jest, surely, all of this. A game played by the Alfur at humanity's expense. Why else was she still here, when everyone she'd ever loved was dead. Why else would they spare Johanas's life, only to condemn him to the same fate as their mentor. He would spend the next decades watching gladiator after gladiator pass through the complex, all of them doomed, destined to meet their end on these harsh sands.

At least Hawk would be spared that fate. At least it would all end for her, one day.

But that end would not come at the hands of the so-called Battleboar.

And so she laughed, the sound ringing from the stands. One by one, then all at once, the crowd fell silent. They stared at the madwoman who dared mock their mighty gladiator, who dodged and ducked the terrible blade, but never came close to finding a mark. She knew what they were thinking, that surely she must be insane, her mind broken...

...and yet as the bout progressed, still she danced. Still she laughed.

She could see the doubt as it blossomed in Battleboar's eyes, the fear that despite all his mighty strength, he had failed to find his mark. Hawk supposed the ferocity of his assault and the enormous weapon had been more than a match for his previous opponents. Probably, that was why the Alfur had matched them, thinking the giant would dispatch her with ease. If so, they proved yet again their naivety in the ways of battle.

The less experienced gladiators might have tried to block Battleboar's terrible swipes with shield or sword, but Hawk hadn't been born yesterday. Even before the gladiator complex and Marcus Aureli, she'd learned to fight on the streets of Goma. Her every day had been a battle to survive—such was the way of life for a pair of orphans without a home.

Or at least, that had been their life, until the rebellion had taken them in...

A growl rumbled from Hawk's throat as the memories flashed in her mind. Jasmine had had a kindly face. A softly spoken voice you could trust. They'd only known her a few weeks, but to the rebellion...she had been their commander and leader, the one they had looked to for hope and inspiration, the mother figure over the fledgeling organisation...

...all of it had been a lie, betrayed the moment she'd stabbed her brother through the back.

Red-hot pain flared across Hawk's shoulder, tearing her from the memory. She stumbled, surprised to find blood dripping down her arm. The laughter died on her lips. The bastard had actually managed to cut her. Just a nick, thankfully, or she would be in two pieces by now. But even so...

Hawk turned her steely gaze on Battleboar.

He seemed as surprised as she was. She could see it in his eyes. He stood, mouth wide, frozen as he looked from her to the blood staining the tip of his sword. It should have buoyed him, given him hope. But as he looked back at Hawk, something in her eyes must have warned him. The blood drained from his face.

"I..."

Hawk attacked.

That was the joy of Aureli's training. The man might be long gone and buried, but if he'd drilled one thing into his recruits, it was to prioritise fitness above all else. Until now, Hawk had exerted little energy evading Battleboar's swipes. She'd barely broken a sweat.

Not so the massive Battleboar.

His forehead was already dripping as she attacked. He had used all of his energies in the assault. Now he found his body wanting. With no shield, his giant sword moved sluggishly to respond to her blow. Sparks burst across the sands as their blades clashed for the first time—but now it was Hawk that refused to retreat.

His sword was too slow to block her second strike, and her short sword opened a shallow cut across his chest. The next took a chunk from his arm, another his ear. He screamed with that one, dropping his blade and stumbling back from her, clutching the bloodied side of his face.

She put him out of his misery then, finishing the blow with a clean stab through the giant gladiator's chest. He cut off midscream, eyes widening. A soft sigh whispered from his lips. He slumped against her, Hawk's blade still impaled in his leather armour. His eyes met hers, and she saw the fear there, the uncertainty.

Hawk laughed. Still holding the dying man upright on her blade, she looked up at the silent crowd. "The mighty Battleboar," she whispered to him. "They will have forgotten your name by the morrow."

At that, she released the hilt of her sword and pushed him away from her. There was an audible *thump* as he struck the sands. Hawk wiped a trickle of sweat from her brow. At least he'd made her work for it a little at the end. Then she reached down and tore her blade from his chest and wiped it on his clothing.

The crowd was still silent as Hawk turned and descended the stairs.

Falcon was waiting for her in the depths.

"Happy?" she asked as the woman met her eyes.

Falcon did not respond.

SIX

EXHAUSTION WEIGHED HEAVILY ON RYDIAN AS HE paused at the treeline. The great cat paused alongside him, the rumble of its panting so loud he feared those in the nearby buildings might hear. They had fortified themselves with Light to make the journey so quickly, burning it in their veins day and night as they ran through the untamed jungles of Talamh. Guided always by the holographic map, they had paused only for quick snatches of sleep as the days slid past, uncounted.

Now they finally stood on the threshold of their destination, it was all Rydian could do to keep his eyes open.

A constant buzz of voices carried from the Goman barracks, interspersed by the occasional round of cheering. Rydian surmised it had been a games day. His stomach tied itself in a knot. He wondered if any of his friends had fallen on the blood-stained sands.

But then, could he even consider them his friends

now? Johanas maybe, but he had only the word of Prince Levaanton that the giant gladiator would be spared. It would have come as little surprise to learn the Goman prince had lied.

Then there was Hazel. His mind couldn't begin to process a reunion with the woman. What could he possibly say to her? His mother, whether in her right mind or not, had killed Hazel's brother.

And she had killed Rydian's father.

A flickering of his rage stirred, a reminder that the Haze was not altogether contained. He sensed it at the edges of their minds, pressing against their consciousness, seeking to repossess its prizes.

I do not like the smell of this place, Rydian's companion's silent voice interrupted his thoughts. *It smells of death.*

"Or dead men walking," Rydian replied grimly.

That was the truth none dared mention, but all embraced in this place. That their fates were sealed, that one day they would meet their end on the blade of an enemy gladiator. It was only a matter of time.

So gladiators like Falcon celebrated each victory, every day more that they lived.

And let the young newcomers be damned.

He clenched his fists at the thought. Falcon was why he was here. Not Hazel or Johanas or the other Gomans. Falcon. He needed to set aside his anger with the woman. She had known Aureli best. If there were secrets to be uncovered, she was most likely to know them.

First though, he needed to get her alone.

They waited until well after midnight before the last of revellers fell silent. Only then did they slip from the trees. The leopard stayed at Rydian's side. They'd already tried separating for a time on the journey, to unpleasant results. The distant buzzing of the Haze had quickly grown back to a shriek. They hadn't tried again since.

Crossing the field that separated the buildings of the gladiator complex from the jungle, Rydian couldn't help but recall the long days and nights he'd spent in this place. The fear of his first day here, of facing Falcon's rejection, and the harshness of his fellow recruits. Of knowing that one day, before he was anywhere close to ready, he would need to step out onto the sands of the arena and face another man in a fight to the death.

Bitterness. Despair. Exultation. Those had been the emotions of his first few months here. But somehow, over the prevailing months, this place had become something else to Rydian. Home.

Reaching the ring of buildings, they paused long enough to cast a glance back at the trees. It was strange. He felt exposed away from the trees, standing in the open like this. Moonlight shone above and there was space all around them. too much space. It felt unnatural, after so long in the jungle. Yet there had been a time when it had been those distant trees that had unnerved him, and that this wide open space had reassured him.

He spent only a few moments in the Goman barracks. There was no sign of Falcon amidst the unconscious bodies, nor in her private quarters. Her absence left Rydian frustrated as he slipped back out into the moonlight. Surely Falcon hadn't fallen after all this time. The woman might be a drunk, but she was a formidable warrior, the best of Aureli's former pupils—or so she claimed. She was practically untouchable in the arena. The only opponent she'd feared was Rotin, and Rydian had taken care of the Alfurian gladiator.

Unless Falcon had given up.

That didn't seem like the fiery woman he'd known, but who was he to claim he knew the Goman gladiator? He didn't even know her real name, from before.

He turned his attention to the central building of the complex.

Rydian had to be careful here. While the building was usually empty, there had been occasions when the Alfur visited—mostly on the days before a games, when odd injuries needed to be healed in preparation for the coming bouts. He was fairly certain the festivities in the barracks were the celebration of a games survived, but if Falcon was no longer around...there were no guarantees.

But Rydian wouldn't let the threat of the overlords deter him. He had nothing to fear from a single Alfur now. Only that it might alert the others.

Even so, he treaded softly as he threaded his way through the corridors, seeking out the old rooms Aureli had enjoyed in this complex. He didn't expect to find much, but he couldn't simply give up now. Not after they'd come so far.

The great cat padded softly at his side, its orange eyes aglow with Light as they scanned the darkness. They were both on edge. Rydian felt sluggish after so long spent in the grips of the Light, like his body was no longer quite his own. It was tempting to reach for that source of power again, to cast aside his fatigue, but he resisted. Better to save the power, in case he needed to face the Alfur after all.

Silence hung over Aureli's chamber as he pushed the doors open, revealing the dark room. Rydian shivered as he paused in the doorway, recalling the last time he'd been there. The stench of his mentor's filth. The howling of the hound as it sought to go to Aureli's rescue. The closeness of Hazel...

Beware!

A snarl tore from the great cat as it leapt forward, placing itself between Rydian and the darkness. He acted instantly, Light blooming within, burning from his skin to cast back the dark. Laughter rasped from a soft throat. Movement stirred in the shadows.

There was no clutter now, no leavings of a depressed man or stench of rotting garbage.

Only Falcon, seated at an empty table, an empty bottle of spirits in one hand, half-full glass in the other.

"Hello, Rydian Holt," she said into the quiet of Rydian's shock. "They let you live after all."

SEVEN

Rydian was so startled by Falcon's appearance, he practically tripped over his own feet. Only a wild grab for the doorframe kept him from crashing to the stone floor.

Laughter grated loudly in Rydian's ears. Falcon hadn't moved from her seat. She raised the mug of golden spirits in his direction.

"To good fortune, I guess."

A long moment passed. Rydian stared at the woman. He'd never understood her. She was the best Goman gladiator by a long shot, but she put no effort into her training, didn't care for another soul in this place. Indeed, she seemed to do everything she could to push others away. Yet she had gone with them to help Aureli.

"You don't seem surprised to see me," he said at last. After a final glance around the room, he allowed the Light of his fist to dim a little.

The wooden chair scraped against the stone floor as Falcon pushed herself to her feet. She drained the last of her mug, then tossed it over her shoulder. The sharp *crack* as it shattered was surprisingly muted in the silence of the room. Rydian still flinched.

"I knew you weren't dead. The Alfur would have paraded your body in front of everyone if that had been the case." Her eyes lingered on Rydian's hand of Light. "I managed to piece the rest together." She turned her gaze to the great cat. "Though I'll admit, the feline is somewhat of a surprise."

A rumble came from Rydian's companion. He rested a hand on the big cat's enormous head and it stilled.

"You know why we came here?"

Falcon was still staring at the big cat. "Its bonded, I take it?" she asked absently. "Guess that's why you're still stable. Helps with the pain, right?"

The breath caught in Rydian's throat. "How did you know that?"

In usual fashion, Falcon ignored him. She crossed to a closet in the corner instead and opened it, then reached inside and cracked open a secret compartment within. Suddenly Rydian's heart was racing—until she emerged a moment later with another bottle of golden liquor.

"Found Aureli's stash of the good stuff," she explained, her voice slurring only slightly. Reaching back into the same compartment, she retrieved two fresh glasses. "The Alfur cleared out the rest of his stuff, but they don't seem to get the concept of 'hidden.' Stupid bastards are too honest for their own good, I reckon."

Rydian raised an eyebrow. Falcon swayed on her feet, a grin pasted across her lips, but she made it back to the table without dropping either bottle or glasses.

"You sure you haven't had enough?"

The cold look Falcon flashed him made her answer to that question obvious. She poured them each a glass and then slid one across the table to where Rydian still stood. His eyes lingered on the glass as the woman lifted her own and raised it in cheers.

"Come on, little Mouse," Falcon cackled. "Don't tell me you discovered ultimate power and decided to become *boring.*"

Rydian sighed, but he'd discovered early on in his time here that there was little point in arguing with the Goman champion. Besides, a pounding had started in the back of his head—no doubt the consequences of his excessive use of the Light these past weeks. And Rydian could use a drink after everything he'd been through.

Lifting the glass, he reached across the table and clinked it with Falcon's, then took a swig...

...and almost spat it back out.

"Gods below!" he gasped. "I thought you said that was Aureli's good stuff!"

His eyes were watering and his throat felt as though he'd swallowed liquid fire. Meanwhile, Falcon had already downed her shot in a single swig and was already refilling her glass. She raised an eyebrow at him over the rim of the bottle.

"Did I?" she asked. "Guess I misspoke. I meant his strong stuff." She grinned.

"Unbelievable," Rydian muttered, setting his glass aside.

Falcon snorted. "I needed something to blot out the smell of the pair of you."

Warmth spread to Rydian's cheeks. He had bathed in the occasional river since regaining the better part of his sanity through the bond with the great cat, but hygiene had mostly fallen by the wayside as they raced across the broad jungles of Talamh.

A growl came from his companion, its yellow eyes brightening, but Falcon only waved a hand.

"Relax, Great One, I'm sure you smell wonderful to one of your kind. The comment was mostly directed at Rydian here." She paused, eying the cat. "Though, apologies, I have not asked your name."

Rydian blinked, looking from the cat to Falcon. Were they communicating? It didn't seem so on his companions part—Rydian hadn't heard it speak. But...

You may tell the Light Giver I am called Fatimah.

"Wait, you have a name? Why didn't you mention it?"

Why did you not mention yours, Rydian Holt?

"Oh," Rydian stammered. "I guess...I just thought you knew."

The great cat snorted its amusement.

"If you two are quite done?" Falcon asked. When

Rydian turned back to her, she was busy pouring another glass of the amber liquid.

"Her name is Fatimah."

"Greetings, Fatimah."

Rydian waited a long moment, before he finally blurted out the question he'd been dying to ask.

"Aureli knew about the Light, didn't he..."

The words died on his lips as Falcon turned her cold blue eyes on him.

"Take a seat, Rydian," she said, "you're making me nervous, looming over me like that."

Rydian swallowed, but he sank into the chair across from her. He allowed the Light of his hand to dim further, until only a glint remained to light their faces. Without thinking, he took another sip of his spirits—and spluttered again as the fiery liquid burned.

"Since when do you drink in here?" he asked absently.

"Since the Alfur cracked down on the good stuff," Falcon replied. "The rules have been...stricter since your disappearance. Only ale in the barracks. It's a good thing Aureli had amounted quite the stash, or I'd be on the lookout for some old fashion retribution." She smiled as she said the words, though not in a manner that suggested she was kidding.

Exhaling slowly, Rydian watched the woman across from him. She seemed little changed since the day she'd come to his cell and told him it was his life, or the entire Goman gladiator team. He turned his eyes to her Manus reader. A glint of Light showed it was still active. So much for that theory.

Noticing the direction of his gaze, Falcon lifted her hand and turned her palm towards Rydian, giving him a better look at her Manus reader.

"Was this what you came here for?" she asked. "Because you thought I was like you?"

"I...I don't know what I came here for."

"I bet," Falcon replied wryly. "It was confusing for us as well, back when Aureli first discovered the secret."

Rydian's heart lurched. "You mean I'm right? He did know about the Light?"

"More than any of us," Falcon admitted. "He's the one who discovered the trick with the Manus Readers."

"What?" Rydian came halfway to his feet. "So you did know? Why didn't you tell anyone?"

"You know why," Falcon replied. "Those of us who went down that path...not many returned. Even with familiars like your Fatimah there, it's only a temporary fix."

"The Haze?"

"We thought we could save the world." Falcon's eyes were distant now, far away in some distant path. "When Marcus came to me... He'd found a way to deactivate our Manus readers. We knew it was a secret we had to keep close, that we needed to bide our time, until enough were prepared." She sighed. "So we used it in the arena at first, as practice. Even drawing on just a little Light, enough that we would go unnoticed, we were faster, stronger."

"What happened?"

"Aureli became the champion. Easily." She laughed, the sound hollow in her throat. "I was his girl back then. Him and me and a few others, we were going to take down our alien overlords." She snorted at the memory. "We were so naïve."

"The Alfur found out, didn't they?" Rydian whispered. "What did they—"

"They never found out," Falcon said quietly. "We had it all planned. Aureli was going to challenge Rotin. Show off our true power. When the Alfurian gladiator fell, we would all rise together, and the crowd with us. The Alfur would fall in a day." She shook her head. "But we didn't understand the Haze."

Rydian swallowed. "Did Aureli…"

"Snap?" Falcon gave a curt shake of her head. "Davis was first. Middle of a training session, he just started attacking everyone around him. Killed half a dozen Riesorans. That's when they made us start training apart. Took three of us, even with the Light, to put him down.

A lump lodged in Rydian's throat as he stared into the woman's eyes, and finally saw the pain there. The agony that had cut her to the core, sliced away all optimism or hope for the future. She had tried once, thought she could change the world, and failed.

Falcon topped up her glass yet again, then slid the bottle across the table for Rydian. This time he drank without hesitation. It was one thing, hearing about his fate from one of the

Alfur. They were the enemy, and had every reason to lie to him. But Falcon...he could see the truth in her pain. He might have saved himself from Rotin's blade in the arena, but this power he had unlocked had doomed him just as surely.

"Afterwards, the Alfur must have suspected something," Falcon continued. "By then Aureli had reactivated our Manus readers, so we weren't discovered, but...it didn't take long for us to realise it wasn't an isolated incident."

Rydian clenched his fists as he listened to her story. He knew well the hope Falcon and Aureli and the other gladiators had felt—and the crushing blow to have it stolen away again. Even now, with Fatimah seated at his side, he could feel the screaming of the Haze at the edges of his mind, prickling his consciousness.

"So what?" he whispered. "That was it? You just gave up?"

"Our options were limited," Falcon sighed, her fingernails tapping gently against her glass. "To continue with our plan would have meant madness and death. We couldn't win, not with those conditions. Most of us reactivated our Manus readers and tried to forget we'd ever held the power to destroy the Alfur in our hands." She looked up then, meeting Rydian's eyes. "But not Aureli."

Rydian swallowed. "All that time?"

"He was a stubborn man. He refused to become a slave again, to live a life ruled by the whims of the Alfur. Even if it cost him his mind. I don't know how he coped, truth be told. Princess helped, though that was another of his gambles."

"He told me a story about the hound," Rydian murmured. "About our ancestors befriending the beasts of this planet."

Falcon nodded. "At least some of the legends are true," she said, her eyes distant.

The hairs on Rydian's neck stood on end. So she didn't know everything. He didn't correct her though. If Levaanton had truly been telling the truth about his people's past, that they had been little better than beasts before the Alfur had come...let Falcon and the others continue to believe they had been greater than that.

Though...perhaps there was more to this story than he'd realised. Aureli *had* bonded with the hound, and he with the great cat at his side. His heart pulsed with sudden home. Maybe that meant there was truth in the old stories after all, that perhaps *something* had existed before the Alfur.

"Imagine our surprise when Aureli waltzed into the barracks with that thing," Falcon continued after a break. "I swear, I saw grown men soil themselves that day. Most thought he'd gone mad. But Princess seemed to help him."

"I was on the brink when I found Fatimah." Rydian drew in a breath. "But you said the effect was only temporary?"

"In a manner," Falcon replied. "Aureli never stopped looking for a real cure. Some way to liberate us all. But

Princess was the closest he ever got. And the bond's beneficial effects wore off the more he used the Light."

His heart stilled. "What?"

The champion's eyes narrowed. "How much Light have you been using?"

"We've been burning it constantly over the last week," Rydian admitted. "We didn't want it to take a month to reach the complex."

"That wasn't your most intelligent decision."

"We'll take a break for a few days—"

"Doesn't work that way," Falcon interrupted. "It's more of a...cumulative effect." She waved a hand. "Difficult to explain. You need to think of it like...a cup!"

She picked up her glass and the bottle of spirits. "Imagine Light is our fine liquor here. Each time you use it, you pour a little more into the cup." Falcon began to pour to illustrate the point. "Now, let's say you stop." Looking him dead in the eye, she did so. "And wait. Give yourself a break. It doesn't change how much is in the cup. So when you use it again, when you start to pour..."

She mimicked the action, until the glass began to overflow onto the table.

"Take my point? I hope so. I'd rather not waste any more of the good stuff."

"You keep saying good stuff..."

Falcon shrugged. "Truth be told, I haven't got much sense of taste left after all these years."

Rydian sighed and put them back on track. "So what are you saying?"

"Once the cup overflows, there's no going back. The pain, the anger, the screaming, it all comes rushing back. You might be able to cope for a while longer, but sooner or later, it will break you..." she paused, casting a deliberate glance at Fatimah. "Break you both."

The big cat rumbled her discontent.

Rydian levered himself to his feet. Images of the night Aureli had died flashed through his mind. Of the stench of this room. Of the howling of Princess in her cave. Of Aureli, stumbling away through the jungle, unable to take the pain any longer.

A tremor came from within him. A tickle of pain. He couldn't tell whether it was remembered, or the first signs of the Haze's return.

"It doesn't matter," he gasped, swinging back on Falcon. His breath came in ragged gasps. "None of it matters. We only need a few of us to bring them down."

"If only it were that simple, kid," Falcon snorted. "You might feel invincible in the grips of the Light, but we are far from it."

"Prince Levaanton seemed to fear me well enough."

"I'm sure. I don't doubt you could have done a lot of damage. But the Alfur have ships capable of levelling entire cities. If he had wanted you dead, you would be."

"Then help me," he hissed, swinging on her. "Help me fight them. Help me recruit others. Help me *win*."

Her laughter surprised him. His head jerked up as she rose from her chair, swaying far more violently than usual. She was well and truly drunk. "Aureli asked me the same thing once," she said, slurring her words now. "You aren't half as cute." She laughed again, the sound harsh in the gloom of the dead man's quarters. "You're both fools. You'll find no help from me, Rydian Holt."

Silence stretched between the two as they faced each other. Rydian clenched his fist, sensing the Light gathering there. He wanted to hate her, to damn Falcon for refusing him. For despoiling the legacy Aureli had left to them.

But he had felt the agony of the Haze. He could understand her fear.

And so all he could muster was pity for the Goman champion.

"And what about *your* Manus reader?" he asked at last.

Falcon pursed her lips. "I'm a coward, kid," she said simply. "I had that thing fixed before Davis's body hit the ground."

"That's why you drink."

Her eyes narrowed. A shadow crossed her face. "I think it's time for you to leave."

"Marcus would be ashamed."

This time when Falcon laughed, there was mirth in her voice. "Marcus was always ashamed of me," she replied, "but Marcus is dead. Only the living get to judge."

"Isn't that the truth."

Rydian spun as a new voice spoke from the doorway.

He froze when he saw who stood there.

Hazel.

EIGHT

Hazel's heart was pounding so loudly in her ears that she could hardly think. She couldn't stop shaking. Couldn't keep the blade in her hand from trembling. It took everything she had not to just leap across the room and drive it through Rydian's black heart.

Surely then the screaming in her head would stop? Surely then she would have peace.

Instead, she held herself in check.

She'd woken in the middle of the night, as she often did these days. Sleep was a fragile, fickle thing now. It only took the slightest of disturbances to wake her.

So it wasn't unusual when she'd found herself alert in the darkness. This time though, there'd been something different about the darkness. The barracks were far from silent, filled with the soft snores of her fellow gladiators—Johanas worst of all.

Yet there had been something else beneath the

rumbling. A silence beyond the creaking of the building. The whisper of promise on the breeze. It was as though the night were expectant, waiting for something.

Agitated, Hazel had abandoned her bed and slipped out into the night, taking her gladius as a matter of habit. Ever since they'd followed Aureli into the jungle and been forced to slay his hound, she hadn't left the buildings of the complex without her blade at her side.

As she'd slipped from the barracks, she had spotted a shadow moving across the grounds. At first she'd thought it Falcon. The woman slept almost as little as her. But no, there had been something about this shadow that called to her, that begged Hazel investigate.

And so she had followed it through the night. She'd lost it in the central complex, slipping between the long corridors and chambers. But eventually, the sound of voices had drawn her here to the chambers of Marcus Aureli. To a room steeped in memories.

And Rydian Holt.

He had come to his feet at her appearance. Standing at the table, eyes wide, she could almost remember he had been her friend, had stood beside her against Falcon and gladiators and the Alfur themselves.

Almost.

"What are you doing here?" Her voice shook, though she'd meant to scream the words.

Rydian flinched all the same. "Hazel..."

A shadow shifted at his side, a light brightened. Breath hissed between Hazel's teeth as she saw the leopard. Her blade cut air as she jerked it towards the creature. A rumble came from deep in its throat and its eyes seemed to burn in the gloom.

"Fatimah, don't," Rydian spoke gently as he rested a hand on the beast's head. "She's a friend."

Hazel swallowed as she looked from the beast to Rydian. Her hand tightened on the hilt of her blade. "Give me one reason why—"

"This," Rydian said gently.

He raised his hand. Only, it wasn't a hand. Its glow had been muted, so that she thought the glow came only from his Manus reader. Now power flared, revealing a hand fashioned from Light itself. It bathed their faces with its raw power, seeming at once liquid and a solid, tangible thing.

She swallowed. The threat in his words was clear to her. Somehow, Rydian had control of the Light. What had he done to receive such a gift from the Alfur? Her fist clenched tighter still around her sword. It didn't matter. She would put him down all the same.

"You should not have returned, Rydian," she rasped.

"Yet I have."

"What do you want?"

"Revenge."

Rage freed Hazel from the grips of her fear. "At least we have that much in common," she spat. "Come on then, draw your blade..." she trailed off. Rydian wore no weapon.

"We don't have to do this, Hazel."

"I think that we do."

"Of course you do!" Falcon laughed. She stumbled forward, her pupils dilated from drink, bottle clutched in one hand. "Let's go outside," she continued, her voice slurring. "Decide this like real gladiators, hey?" she paused, giving Rydian a strange look. "I want to see what this one can do."

A frown creased Rydian's forehead. He stared at Falcon for a long moment. Hazel wondered what the woman was to him.

"Very well," he said finally.

Without another word, he walked past Hazel out into the corridor. She let him go, lingering in the room with Falcon.

"Last chance, girl," the Goman champion said, her eyes suddenly far clearer than before.

"I don't remember asking you," Hazel snarled.

She stalked after Rydian before the woman had a chance to reply.

Hazel found her former friend standing on the sands of the practice grounds. The great cat stayed close to his side. Its enormous yellow eyes watched her approach. She suppressed a shiver. The thing was even more unnerving than Aureli's hound.

Rydian's eyes were fixed on the sand at his feet, which glinted strangely in the Light of his hand.

"Well?" he asked, his head jerking up to look at her.

"Where is your weapon?"

"Here," Falcon said, drawing her own blade and tossing it to the former gladiator.

Rydian caught it without hesitation, then raised his eyebrows and started to turn towards Hazel. "Are you sure—"

Hawk attacked.

In that moment, every moment of pain, every agony and frustration and loss she had experienced over the last year burned to the surface.

Her blade flashed for Rydian's throat. For a second, she didn't think he would defend himself. Even the great cat seemed to have been caught off-guard. But at the last minute, the blade in his hand flashed up, and steel met steel.

Sparks flashed and Hawk's arm jarred. She staggered, but only for a second. Her feet moved nimbly in the loose sands. Spinning, she hacked a cut at the space she expected Rydian to be standing.

He wasn't there.

Instead, he bounded backwards. A single leap carried him halfway across the training arena. He raised his sword as he landed, the Light from his hand pulsing gently in the moonlight. There was no smile now, no signs of amusement. His blue eyes watched her in the twilight.

"We don't have to do this, Hazel," he said again.

Hawk's snarl was more animal than human. She crossed the ground in an instant and attacked again. Her weapon flashed for Rydian's face, his groin, his chest, relentless. Each he turned aside with a flick or a twist of his blade. They wore no shields, but Rydian remained relaxed, almost casual in the way he defended, as though he knew where her attacks would come from before Hawk did herself.

It didn't matter.

With each swing of her sword, she saw again her brother's face, the surprise in his eyes as Jasmine's blade plunged through his back, as its bloody point erupted from his chest.

And she saw the calm eyes of Rydian's mother. They had seemed to watch Hawk, even as the woman tore the blade from her brother and cast him aside. Even as the Aflurian guards had burst into the room. Even as the Light of half a dozen Manus readers had extinguished her fellow rebels.

"Why didn't you die!"

She didn't know whether she screamed it at Rydian, or Jasmine Holt, or even herself. That was the truth of her pain, a terrible guilt that *she* had survived, when everyone else that night had perished. It was enough that some nights she wondered whether Aureli had been right, if she should just walk into the jungle one night and be done with it. At least then she might finally have peace.

Only something inside her refused to surrender so easily, to allow her light to be snuffed out.

So she fought, and prayed for someone with the strength to finally strike her down.

Finally she stepped back from Rydian, panting heavily in the humid night air. "Why won't you fight back!"

"I didn't come here to fight you, Hazel," he replied, his face hard. "I came here in search of a way to destroy the Alfur, to free our people." He lowered his sword. "But if this is what you must do, I won't stop you." He tossed the weapon aside.

"I will!"

Hawk advanced. Rydian didn't move as she placed the blade to his throat. Their eyes met, and she saw the determination there, that he would not back down. And something else...pain? A tremor swept through her. She pressed the blade harder, until a line of blood dripped down Rydian's throat.

"Well?" she hissed. "Any last words?"

Rydian stared back. "I am sorry for what happened to your brother."

Another tremor shook Hawk. She saw again the moment her brother had fallen, saw the wild eyes of Jasmine as she stood over his body. So like her son. Now she knew the truth, Hazel wondered how she'd ever missed it.

"Fight me, damnit!" she screamed.

"No," Rydian said.

Another image flashed before Hawk's eyes. Of an old man falling to her blade, his life's blood staining the sand. And Rydian beside him, sobbing, begging, pleading for him to stay.

"I killed him," she rasped, "your father. I deserve it."

Held in place by her blade, Rydian didn't move, but

she sensed the sudden tension in him. She gathered herself, ready to resume the fight...

"No," Rydian said, "No, the only ones that deserve death are the Alfur."

It was too much. A scream tore from her throat...and suddenly she was Hazel again. She hurled the blade away from her. Sobbing, she sank to her knees. Again and again she saw the old man fall, the blood dripping from her blade. The weight of that deed had weighed on her ever since, crippling her, corrupting her. How could she ever forgive herself for what she'd done, for slaying an innocent old man?

And yet...Rydian stood there, offering forgiveness.

Sand crunched as he knelt alongside her. She felt his hand on her shoulder.

"We'll have our revenge, Hazel," he whispered. "On all of them. Together."

NINE

Lounging in her quarters, Serena stared at the glass on the table before her. The room's illumination had dimmed with nightfall. But it was not dark. The glow of flames came through the window on the other side of the room. The humans, rioting again. And they didn't even know what the princes had planned for them.

Then there was the other source of Light. The glass. Its shimmering glow lit up a circle around Serena, casting back the gloom of night. Resisting the flickering violence of those distant fires. That Light represented all that was glorious about her people. With its power thrumming in their veins, they had no need to kill, to consume the flesh of others. Just the thought made her flesh crawl. Barbaric. Yet it was the fate of every other lifeform on this planet.

But it was more than just food to the Alfur. It was the source of the inhuman strength. It powered their glorious technologies, had sent them to the stars and across galaxies, brought them to this place.

It was also a lie.

For the Alfur could not produce Light on their own. Once, before they had come to this place, before the Haze had trapped them on Talamh, her father claimed they'd had ways of creating Light. But here, surrounded by the Haze, cut off from the rest of the galaxy, from their people, there was only one source of Light great enough to fuel the hunger of her people.

Humanity.

"You should eat, Serena."

She looked up as a voice came from the doorway. Her father stood there. She hadn't seen him since that fateful meeting. Too busy, he'd claimed through their Manus readers. Now Aiden Levaanton looked weary, his skin pallid, missing the usual sheen of the royal families. Even his golden eyes had dimmed.

"Father." Despite his obvious exhaustion, Serena offered no concession in her greeting. "So nice of you to finally visit."

Her father gave an audible sigh as he crossed the room and joined her in the glow of the Light.

"I have been otherwise occupied," he said, seating himself at the table across from her.

"Planning a genocide, I know," she replied curtly.

"It is a mercy—"

"Please," she interrupted, her voice suddenly soft.

"Speak your lies amongst the council, but do not bring them here, Father."

He said nothing for a moment, though his lips were pursed as though in thought. "I am told you have not been feeding," he said at last.

She rolled her eyes. "Who told you that?"

It was only a half truth. An Alfur who forsook their daily intake of Light quickly withered and became...a lesser version of themselves. Serena had only limited her intake to rations to match the rest of the tower.

"Does it matter?" Aiden's voice carried a long-suffering tone. "Why don't you humour an old Alfur and prove the rumours wrong?"

Serena's eyes turned to the Light. She had pieced the truth together from what the other heirs had told her. The true reason for the cull. Their refinement process was compromised. With the Haze growing ever more power-ful, fed by the violent emotions in the riots across Talamh, the Manus readers could no longer extract sufficient Light to meet Alfurian demands.

That was what the council feared. Or so she thought.

"How much blood will our survival cost, Father?" she asked at last, turning her golden eyes on the prince. "How many must die so that the Alfur can prevail?"

Aiden Levaanton stared back at her for a long while. Finally though he blinked, and looked away.

"A third," he said, so quietly she almost lost the words in the darkness. But he said them again, and the second time there was steel in his voice. "We have decided on a third of the population."

Serena felt the Light flush to her face. Shock. That was her first emotion. The glow of her surprise shone from her skin and her father went on before she could respond.

"I argued for less. Sandoval and Hassan wanted half, and Zavala was very nearly with them. Your friend Nate and I managed to swing him to our side, thankfully."

Her father babbled on. Serena stared at him, hardly listening to what he was saying. *A third.* How many millions would that be? She had expected the blood toll to be heavy, had steeled herself for it, preparing to argue for a better path. But *a third?* She was speechless.

"Stop," the word burst from her at last, catching her father mid-sentence. Mouth open, he froze, staring at her. "Just stop," she whispered. Her eyes slid closed and she drew in a breath, struggling to gather her shattered thoughts. "How?" she said at last. "How can you go along with this?"

"Because I must," her father growled. His head came up, a fire lighting in his eyes. "All I do is for our people. Even were I forced to kill each and every one of those thirty million humans with my own bare hands, I would do it gladly for you, for my Alfur."

"So says the soldier," Serena spat, "but will and need are different, Father. We pretend to be a civilisation of knowledge, but no species of wisdom would condone your plan. They would seek a better way."

"And what is this better way, Daughter?" Levaanton replied, his voice suddenly soft, the fire vanished as quickly as it had appeared. Sat before her again was the Alfur of age, of exhaustion. "Pray tell, what miracle of the stars would you pin the survival of our species upon?"

Serena swallowed as she met her father's eyes. She thought he might actually be earnest, might be looking for a way out. It had to be worth the gamble.

"On the humans, Father," she whispered at last. "You and our ancestors that first came here, you must have seen something within them, to raise them up, to grant them the gift of sentience. In all the time since, we have watched them grow, guiding them. Helping them to become something *more.* But now the time has come to trust them to stand on their own feet. To grant them their freedom."

She trailed off, watching her father for some response. He said nothing for the longest time. Eyes fixed on some place over her shoulder, he seemed a thousand lightyears away, on another world, another time. Finally though, he blinked, and the golden irises fixed on his only daughter.

"No, Serena," he whispered. "I wish it could be so, but that cannot be."

"Why not?" Serena said quickly. "Please, father, open your eyes. Imagine, humanity and the Alfur, working together. See what they have become in just a few short centuries." Her words grew more rushed as her mind ran away with the possibilities. "Imagine, their ingenuity, guided by Alfurian wisdom, surely we could finally solve the problems that have marooned us here, could unravel the Haze that torments the creatures of Talamh—"

"*No!*" Her father's sudden shout took Serena by surprise.

Suddenly he was on his feet, fists clenched, Light boiling beneath his translucent flesh. Serena rose by instinct, Light gathering in her own Manus reader by way of reflex. A wave of nausea swept over her though—she still had not replenished herself with the Light on the table. She swayed, stars suddenly dancing before her eyes.

Her father seemed to notice her distress. His Light died as quickly as it had appeared. He stepped forward and placed a hand on her shoulder, guiding her back to the chair. For once, Serena allowed it to happen. Damn but she had grown used to that extra Light she'd enjoyed as a gladiator.

"Here," Aiden said, his voice soft as he pushed the glass of Light towards her.

Serena shivered as she looked down at its glow. The power of worlds, but attained at such cost. She drank quickly, before her mind could linger too long on other thoughts. The effect was instantaneous, the sudden brightening of her skin, the stars dying from her eyes. Mind refreshed, she looked back to Aiden Levaanton.

"Why can it not be so, Father?" she whispered.

He pursed his lips. "I...I wish you could understand, Daughter. That you could have seen...but no, that is a curse I would wish upon no Alfur." A shake of his head dismissed her question. "For once, let it be enough to accept your elders know better."

"I will never accept that," she snapped. "Not when you openly condone genocide. How can you be so short sighted? You think the humans that remain will accept this? That they will not hate us with every inch—"

"*Enough!*"

The words died on Serena's lips as her father rose, his face a thunder cloud, his eyes crackling with the power of his rage. She held her breath, waiting to see whether his ironlike restraint would crack further. After a long moment, he exhaled and turned from her, as though to leave.

"You will doom us all," she said to his back.

"I said enough, Serena," this time Aiden Levaanton's voice was a whisper. "You will find no support for your human sympathies. Not after your last display in the arena. These creatures are a threat to all of us."

"They could be an opportunity."

"You do not understand—"

"Oh, I understand," Serena hissed. Now it was her turn to rise and stride after her father. Light burned beneath her skin, reaching every inch of her chambers. "Did I not witness their power with my own eyes? Almost perished because of it. Yet it was the human who spared me. Who left our city willingly, without unleashing the death and destruction you so fear." Drawing in a breath, she came to a stop before her father. "He spared my life, Father. How can we not do the same for his people?"

"Because we were lucky." Came his reply. "Because the next time may not be the same."

"Very well," Serena rasped. She lifted her chin to meet his eyes. "Then now that I am healed, I will be returning to the arena."

It was a weak show of resistance, a petty rebellion against his absolute power. Yet it was all she had left.

"No," Aiden Levaanton said, his voice low, exhausted. Yet inexorable. "I forbid it."

"Just try and stop me."

Again his eyes flickered closed. It struck her then how exhausted he was. How old he had become, this prince that had ruled her people in Goma for centuries. Not eldest, but close. Always before, he had seemed so calm, so in control. Now he seemed strung out, almost broken.

"So be it." His words took Serena by surprise.

He waved a hand, and the doors to her chambers hissed open. Two Alfur stepped into her room.

"Since you love your human culture so much, we will adapt a piece of it for you," her father said quietly. "From now until the cull is complete, you are under house arrest, daughter. You will not leave your chambers. You will not visit your friends or fellow heirs. Your duties will be completed by others." He stared at her for a long moment, eyes burning. "A good Alfur would not need guards to ensure their obedience, but I fear your obsession with humanity has corrupted you. Perhaps some time of quiet contemplation will help you rediscover our principles."

With that, Aiden Levaanton turned and strode from

the room. The pair of guards stood awkwardly in the doorway a moment, looking from her to each other, before retreating through the doors. They closed with a hiss.

And Serena Levaanton was left alone in the silence of her quarters.

TEN

The grass was cool on Rydian's bare feet as he
moved through the steps of the sword dance. It was a
simple combination of blocks and strikes, something
Aureli had only just begun to teach him before the man's
untimely end. It had been something Rydian thought
forgotten, or only partially remembered, until his bond
with Fatimah.

Now he saw each individual move as clearly as the day
Aureli had taught it.

More than that, actually. With the Light thrumming
in his veins, Rydian could see the pathways the pattern
was supposed to open. Modes of combat beyond the basic
strikes, as though Aureli had taught him the foundation to
a much greater dance.

After half an hour, he began to expand on that foundation, and soon found himself leaping and spinning, his
body moving as an extension of his mind, of the Light

within. And he wondered, what had Aureli taught him? This was no weapon for gladiators, a solo dance between two vicious opponents. As he spun, striking down one imaginary opponent after another, he began to wonder...

...had Aureli taught him this, or something else?

Rydian came to a halt. Puffing slightly, he looked around.

The shadows of morning had found him in the open field at the edges of the complex. In the depths of his trance, he'd imagined the shadows his enemy. Strangely, they had not been Alfur, but a faceless, unknown entity. He wondered at that, and the dance of death he'd practiced. He had gone far beyond anything Aureli had taught him. Where had that come from? There had been an ancient quality to the display, as though this were some part of his heritage, some dance of war passed down to him by ancient ancestors.

It made no sense. Even had he known any ancestor beyond his parents, there was nothing ancient about humanity on Talamh. The Alfurian prince had made that quite clear. Unless this dance was some remnant of animalist creatures that had been humanity before their arrival.

"Rydian."

His thoughts were broken by a voice. He froze, heart suddenly racing, before he allowed himself a grin. Turning, he looked Johanas up and down.

"Did you get bigger?"

A laugh like thunder rang across the field as Johanas swept Rydian into a bone crunching hug.

"It's true!"

Blinking back tears, Rydian hugged his friend back. He had made demands of the Alfur, commanded them to spare his friends...but until this moment, he'd dared not believe their promises. Johanas had caused a riot, after all, and the Alfur weren't known for their forgiveness. At least this proved there was a modicum of honour amongst the Alfur.

"Seriously, you're looking well, Johanas," he said as they broke apart. "Or is it still Bloodlust?"

The grin slipped from his friend's face. "Never again," he said grimly. "It will be Johanas until the end of my days."

"As it should be. Hazel told me you do not fight any longer."

"You've...ah, seen her?"

Rydian grimaced. "Yeah. It went about as well as you'd expect."

"Since you're in one piece, I'll count it as a win."

"Barely," Rydian muttered, then smiled. "It's good to see you, my friend. Really."

"Why do I sense there is a but?" Johanas asked, raising eyebrow.

Rydian pursed his lips. "Because we might yet need Bloodlust if we're to save the world."

A second eyebrow joined the first. "Your aspirations have come a long way since last we saw one another."

"Having a doomsday clock ticking above your head will do that, sadly," Rydian replied. He shook his head. "I'm not saying anything is fixed in stone yet. Only...I have a way of fighting back now, a new power. First though, I need to find a way of avoiding the consequences."

Johanas was silent for a long time. They stood together in the emerald sunlight, two friends that had fought together, bled for one another. Recalling the first day they had met, how Johanas had struggled, how he had mourned the blood he'd spilt, Rydian knew what he would one day ask of the man was too steep a price to pay for anyone.

He would ask it anyway.

"My father was always a pacifist because he knew there could be no victory against the Alfur." He paused. "But if you tell me, Rydian Holt, that there is a way to fight back, then...then I am with you."

Relief swept through Rydian. After Falcon's rejection, he'd feared Johanas would be much the same—if for very different reasons. Smiling, he held up his fist, allowing its Light to brighten.

"This will show us the way, I hope."

Johanas chuckled. "I had meant to ask you about that. We've all heard the rumours. What really happened, against Rotin?"

"Well, this..." Rydian replied. "She took my hand, but gave me something...else."

"She?"

"Yes," Rydian nodded absently. "I unmasked her." He

shook himself and looked again at his friend. "The Alfur have been lying to us."

He told the giant gladiator everything then. About the Light within each of them, and how Aureli and Falcon and others had learned to use it. The power it could grant them. And the cost it exacted on the wielder. About the Haze.

Everything, except that dark secret the prince had told him. That their history was a lie. That everything they knew of their world before the Alfur had come was a fairy tale.

Rydian had decided days ago he would take that secret to his grave.

When he'd finished, Johanas looked at his own Manus reader. The steel cylinder glowed gently from the crystal embedded at its core. That Light was just a fraction of Johanas's true power. Of all their power. The untold potential of humanity had been locked away by the Alfur, binding them to the overlords. A steep price to pay for their sanity. But the question remained, would the price of their freedom be steeper still?

"What is it like?" Johanas asked at last.

"Like there's a fire burning inside me," Rydian answered immediately. He looked around and found Fatimah lying in the shadows of a nearby building. The leopard stirred at his attention, a rumble coming from its chest as it rose on legs. "It was worse, before I found her."

Some of the colour drained from Johanas's face as he

noticed the big cat. He cast an uneasy glance at Rydian. "Is it...ah, safe?"

Laughter came from the nearby buildings. Hazel appeared, her face grim. "Hardly," she said, crossing the grass to where they stood.

"She's harmless." Rydian grinned.

"I'm sure she's many things. I doubt harmless is one of them."

Johanas hesitated, looking from one to the other, then shrugged. "Well, she's certainly an improvement on Aureli's hound."

Silence fell between them. This was the first time they'd all been together since that day in the arena, when Johanas had made his own stand against the Alfur. When he'd refused to fight, to kill—even if it meant his own death. And they had come to support him.

So much had passed since that day, it seemed a hundred years ago now. Yet Rydian felt a peace within that they were all alive, that somehow they had beaten the odds. Even if things could never be the same.

"So, what's the plan?" Hazel asked at last.

Rydian grinned. "We're going back to Goma, of course."

"I'm sure the Alfur will have something to say about that."

"I wasn't intending on asking their permission," he said grimly. "Before I left, Rotin told me something. About my mother, and what the resistance were seeking in the Alfurian temple. She implied it might be something that could help us fight back. Maybe a weapon, maybe something to do with the Haze."

"And you trust it?" Johanas asked, his brow furrowed.

"Of course not," Hazel said through clenched teeth. Her eyes burned as she looked at Rydian. "Right? Please tell me you're not going to base all our plans off the word of an Alfur?"

Rydian hesitated at the fury in her words, but he could not back off now. There options were limited. "I am," he said. "She says she's on our side. I'm not sure why. Maybe it's because I spared her life—"

"*What?*" The pair exclaimed in unison, before Hazel went on: "You realise 'she' has killed hundreds of us, right? Butchered us like dogs in the arena, all for her own amusement?"

"I know," Rydian met her eyes. "And maybe I should have killed her. But then I would be dead, and the truth about the Light would have never reached you. So let's just forget that for a moment—"

"Yes, let's get back to the part where you want to put all our hopes on one of the Alfur," Hazel snapped."

Rydian closed his eyes, suddenly weary. "Not all our hopes," he rasped. Opening his eyes again, he faced the fiery gladiator. "I could raze it all to the ground. Free a few gladiators, launch an attack the next games, destroy their towers, chase the Alfur from the surface of this planet."

"I like that plan," Hazel said with passion.

"And drive ourselves insane," Rydian pointed out. "Which is why I'm calling it plan B. First, we investigate this other lead. The resistance was interested enough in the rumours to risk themselves."

"It was a trap, Rydian," Hazel rasped. "I know you don't believe she could—"

"I believe you, Hazel," Rydian cut her off. He swallowed, eyes burning as he imagined his mother... "I believe mom discovered something beneath that place," he continued, rasping out the words. "Something that unleashed her own Light, exposed her to the Haze. Maybe something we can harness, and use against the Alfur." He sighed. "I know, it's not much to go on. But it's all I've got."

"Then it's what we'll do," Johanas stepped in before Hazel could say more. He met Rydian's eyes, then Hazel's. "Together."

Rydian nodded his thanks. A moment later, Hazel did the same.

"There's just one problem," Johanas continued. "The Alfurian temple was in Goma. We're not."

"That's why I came here," Rydian explained. "To catch a ride."

Johanas grunted. "Alright, there are...a number of problems with your plan," he said, "sorry, I was just being polite, but...it's really more of an outline, than and actual plan, Rydian."

Rydian raised an eyebrow.

"Did you want a list?" Johanas asked. When Rydian only crossed his arms expectantly, he rolled his eyes. "Fine." Raising a hand, he began to tick off points. "How do you get to the city? When you get there, how do you find wherever they've stashed this secret weapon—because they're bound to have moved it. If you *do* find it, how will you use it? We don't even know what it does—"

"Okay, okay, okay!" Rydian exclaimed. "I get it. I told you, I'm not going on much. But I have to do *something*."

"I'm not saying we shouldn't," Johanas said, offering a gentle smile.

"Then what *are* you saying?"

"That we need more information."

"Obviously."

Johanas chuckled. "Well, couldn't this Rotin tell you more, if she's really on our side?"

"Obviously," Rydian replied, irritation prickling at him. "Maybe if we get to Goma, I can find her and ask some more..."

"Yes," Johanas replied, nodding in an exaggerated manner. "Or, you know, and I'm just spit-balling here—you could use your incredible newfound powers to contact her."

Rydian blinked.

ELEVEN

The Alfur did not punish their children. There was no need. Not amongst a species where civil disobedience and crime was practically blasphemy. What need was there for time outs or incarceration for a people whose greatest transgressions were...Serena couldn't think of a single crime committed in her long years of life.

Well, amongst themselves at least. Crimes against humanity was another matter.

So it was that Serena's newfound restrictions were an altogether novel experience.

And mind bogglingly frustrating.

Lying on her bed staring up at the perfectly white metal ceiling, she wondered how humans did it. She already knew how many joints had been placed into the steel panels to hold it all together. She'd also counted every Light emitter, ticked off every dot in the panelled walls. She was of half a mind to start counting the threads of her sheets. If things did not change soon, she would surely go insane.

Yet at any given moment, thousands of humans were incarcerated in the Goman slums, locked away as punishment for minor transgressions. Civil disobedience was practically a religion to them, and no amount of punishment by the Alfur seemed to make a difference. Even something as obviously detrimental as unlawful dumping of rubbish was done on a daily basis.

After just a few days of confinement, Serena was close to losing her mind. The experience had given her a whole new level of respect for their supposedly unevolved cotenants on this backwater planet. She could see why some chose the gladiator camps over confinement.

"Gah!"

Just the thought of the arena set her blood to racing. She levered herself from the bed, her frustration threatening to boil over. The past few days had forced her to confront at least one uncomfortable truth.

That she hadn't fought in the arena just to frustrate her father.

She had enjoyed it.

The thrill of combat, the rush of testing her own ability against the finest of humanity. There was a power in that experience, in knowing your life hung by the thread of your own ability. And the humans had constantly challenged her, despite her record over them. Their warriors had grown over the years, until not even the Light flowing in her veins was enough to guarantee victory.

Little wonder she was experiencing some form of withdrawal now.

Serena's only consolation her Manus reader. The other heirs had kept her up to date on events beyond the walls of her chambers. She was trying to organise a resistance—or at least minor opposition—to the cull through them, but so far, their efforts had been frustrated by a population terrified of human expansion.

As though someone had read her thoughts, Serena's implant began to tingle.

"Cassia?" She couldn't keep the excitement from her voice as she recognised the Manus signature of her friend. "What's happening? Do you know a date yet?"

Laughter came through the device. The heat grew in her Manus reader, then a projection of the other Alfur sprung to life beside the bed. The hologram Cassia folded her arms and looked down at Serena still reclining on the pillow.

"Lying down on the job, Serena?"

She snorted. "Hardly."

Her fellow heir cackled softly. "Yes, I suppose there's not much work to be done from prison."

"Hardly prison," Serena muttered. "It's house arrest. I told you, there's a difference..."

"Is there though..." Cassia questioned a broad grin on her lips. "I mean, what's one empty room you can't leave from another?"

"Well, for starters, I don't have to share my shower with a dozen others."

"They truly do that?" Cassia asked, her eyebrows raising into her silver strands of hair. "Barbaric!"

Serena snorted. "It's us *doing* it to them, remember?"

"Yes, I suppose that's right."

Silence fell between them. Serena cleared her throat. "You had news?"

"Oh, yes..." Cassia trailed off for a moment. "It's not *good* news, I'm afraid."

"They set a date." Serena didn't make it a question. She'd been expecting this for a while now.

"Three weeks," Cassia confirmed.

Serena cursed like a human for a full minute. By the time she finished, both Cassia's eyebrows had disappeared into her long fringe.

"Wow. Were there some new ones in there?"

Ignoring her friend's remarks, Serena rose from the bed and began to pace the length of her room. The hologram followed her Manus reader as she moved. It would project her immediate surroundings to Cassia wherever she was, if the other Alfur had her settings right.

"We have to stop them," Serena muttered as she moved.

"Yes, yes, I know." A pause. "But Serena, what can we do? Your father and the council have spoken—"

Serena slumped back to her bed. "I know." Truth be told, she was at a loss herself. "I was hoping maybe *you'd* thought of something."

There was a long, awkward pause from her friend. "Look, Serena, we tried, you know? But the count has already started. Not just in Goma. Every city on Talamh. The ball is already in motion, and most of our people are behind it. They're afraid, Serena. They know what happened in the arena. They can see what's happening below. They want a solution."

Serena closed her eyes. They had already had this conversation, in varying forms, over the past few days.

"Okay," she said at last. "Well, keep in touch. You know where I'll be if you come up with something."

"I know," all trace of humour had left her friend's face now. "Take care of yourself, Serena. I'm not sure our kind are made for imprisonment."

Eyes still closed, Serena nodded. She felt, rather than saw, her friend's presence depart the room. She sighed as the Manus reader in her palm grew cold.

Agitated by their conversation, Serena came to her feet. Feeling the need to refresh herself, she stripped off her underthings and crossed to her wash chambers. The boiling jets of water had become her daily release, a place where she could escape the painstaking tedium, to wash the horror of each fresh development from her skin, if not her mind.

No doubt the long periods beneath the jets were a waste of precious Light in a time of scarcity, but if her father had a problem with her actions he could come and reprimand her himself.

Serena closed her eyes as she stepped into the chamber, the jets activating at a signal from her Manus reader. The waters were heated to boiling, enough to scald a human's flesh, but the Alfur were made of tougher stuff. At least when it came to heat. There was a reason why four of their five cities were situated around the planet's equator. Only poor Boustor, their remote mountain look-out, suffered the chills of winter. But even there, natural thermals beneath Talamh's surface helped to maintain heat within the Aflurian towers.

She could not have said how long she stood beneath the burning waters. Only that a numbness had begun to creep through her skin by the time a tingling in her hand alerted her to another communication. Letting out a sigh, Serena stepped from the waters. Steam billowed around her and she struggled to make out the name of the contact in the projection. She made a gesture to open the voice line.

"Hello?" she asked.

"Ah...is this Rotin?"

Serena jumped at the unfamiliar voice. They seemed to be speaking right into her ear—and far louder than most of her voice communications. Almost as though they were in the room with her. It was unnerving enough that she took a brief second to look around in case anyone had snuck into her chambers.

Don't be a fool. There are guards on the door. And what Alfur would do something so...crass anyway?

She turned her attention back to the device in her hand.

"Who is this?" she asked, moving towards the exit of the bathing chamber. "Why are you calling me Rotin. Everyone knows that's just my arena name..."

She trailed off as realisation struck her. She *did* recognise this voice. But...that was impossible. Her hearts throbbed in sudden panic. Rydian Holt was alive.

And he was looking for her.

"Rotin is the only name that *I* know you by."

The voice came again as she emerged into the Light of her apartment. She looked around again, the thrumming in her core increasing, as though she expected the human to leap out at her at any moment. This was impossible, wasn't it? Humans couldn't connect with Alfurian Manus readers. Their devices were blocked...

...and Rydian didn't even have a device.

"You're alive," she said finally, coming to a halt in the middle of her chamber.

A long pause followed. She began to wonder if she'd heard his voice at all. Or if she had finally struck under the strain. Maybe she'd imagined it. Some desperate, last grasp at hope to go with her looming despair—

"Ah..." Rydian's voice came at last. He sounded hesitant. "Yes...alive. Ahem, yeah...so, I didn't realise this worked with holograms..."

"Wha—"

Serena's eyes widened. Her gaze darted to her palm. The holographic function should be off. But...Rydian wasn't using a Manus reader. His Light had connected directly to her device. All rules were off.

Light flooded to her cheeks, brightening the room, and she was halfway through grabbing the sheets from her bed to wrap around herself before logic took hold. He was only a human. Not even of her own species. The rules of Alfurian decency hardly counted...

Though on the other hand...

Serena finished wrapping the sheets around her torso before turning her attention back to her Manus reader. She made a gesture with her hand that would, under normal circumstances, accept a holographic call. An image of the Goman gladiator sprang to life before her.

The breath caught in her throat when she saw him. The hologram seemed to have more life than the usual affair conjured up by Manus readers, and her cheeks brightened further at the illicit display she'd invertedly given the human. Regardless, he was looking surprisingly healthy for a creature that had spent the better part of a month roaming the jungles of Talamh. Even more so for a human infected by the Haze.

She wasn't mad. Somehow, the human lived.

"Rydian Holt," she said formally. "To what do I owe the pleasure?" She paused, head craning to the side. "You should know, it is considered ill-mannered amongst my people to activate hologram functionality without the other's approval."

"I can imagine," came the reply. "Though, some amongst my people consider it ill-mannered to enslave a sentient species. Let's not get into semantics, shall we?"

Serena snorted despite herself. "Yes, I suppose not. I

must say, I am surprised to find you…in control of your faculties."

"You mean to find me sane?" His voice was tinged with no small amount of bitterness. "Believe me, it was a close thing after your father dumped me in the middle of the jungle."

"I can imagine." She pursed her lips as the silence stretched out. "I don't mean to pry," she said, "but was there a reason you have reached out."

"The clue you gave me about my mother." His response came immediately. Strange, there was usually a delay for communications over greater distances. She hoped this didn't mean he was already in the city. That would be a disaster for everyone involved. "I need to know more."

She might have guessed as much. The clue she had given him had been an impulsive, spur of the moment act. The act of a child, not an heir to the Goman throne.

Saying more now, knowing this Light possessed human had found a way to survive the Haze…it would be downright treason. If Rydian had begun to unlock the secrets of the Light, without losing his sanity, then he presented a terrible threat to her entire species.

She should alert her father immediately.

Her father, who even now plotted to cull millions of humans in the name of peace.

"Please," the emotion in Rydian's voice was shocking after so long in the presence of the carefully controlled Alfur. "I…need something. Anything."

She swallowed. "I am not sure what I can offer you, Rydian Holt," she said. "My interference only ever seems to make things worse. You should forget what I said. Enjoy your newfound freedom."

"My mother discovered something in your temple, didn't she?"

Serena frowned. "Temple?" she asked. That was a peculiar use of their language. "The Alfur do not have a religion."

Silence fell across the room. "Then what was that place my mother broke into."

"I thought it an Enforcer warehouse, where their weapons were kept..."

"If that's so, why were Alfurian ships spotted coming and going?" Rydian queried. "Surely the Enforcers could protect their own weapons."

"I..." the ships were news to Serena. What she'd said was the truth—at least as far as she and the average Alfur were aware. The building the resistance had attacked *was* a weapons outpost for the Enforcers. Nothing particularly powerful—just shock sticks and the like. But that was why her father had come down so hard on the rebels caught there...wasn't it?

"I do not know," she answered at last, truthfully. "Perhaps there is more here than I knew."

"Aren't you a princess or something?"

Serena pursed her lips. "A rebellious heir, would be a better translation. My father does not tell me everything."

Apparently, she added to herself.

"Well this weapons store, or whatever was in there, do you know where it is now?"

"No. Unfortunately, I am not in the best standing, currently, with my father." Her eyes fell to the floor as she felt a wave of embarrassment. "I have been placed on house arrest."

"The Alfur have house arrest?" The human seemed genuinely surprised.

"It is a somewhat novel invention, solely for my benefit."

"Huh." An edge of humour crept into the human's voice. "What did you do?"

"Voiced my objections to the upcoming cull," Serena replied without thinking.

Silence.

"What?"

Serena cursed softly to herself. She'd forgotten the humans did not know.

"The princes have made a decision," she found herself saying. "The human populace has become unwieldy and violent. Their population is to be culled by a third."

A longer silence followed this proclamation. "When?"

"A few weeks from now."

"We have to stop it."

"As I said," Serena replied, her irritation beginning to show. "I have already spoken—"

"To hell with your 'speaking'," Rydian snapped, true anger showing on his holographic face. Light flickered and he seemed to grow larger, taking on some...solidity. "Your people intend to slaughter millions of mine. There is no middle ground here, Rotin. You're either on our side, or an accomplice to mass murder."

This time it was Serena's turn for silence. Despite her power and rank, she found herself unable to meet the human's eyes, to match the smouldering intensity she found there. She stared at the ground instead, struggling for answers, for the words that would make him understand.

There were none to be had.

"I know," she said instead. "I wish there was something I could do."

"There is," the response came immediately this time. "We need to know what was in that temple or outpost or whatever it was. And we need to know where your father moved it."

"I do not know—"

"Then find out, Rotin."

She hesitated, but there was no denying the human's words. "I will try," she said inclining her head in defeat.

"Good," Rydian replied, before his voice took on a softer touch. "Please, Rotin. Do what you can. And thank you for the warning."

Serena swallowed, feeling suddenly awkward at the end of the conversation. She was still wrapped in only a sheet. It shouldn't have mattered, yet feeling the human's eyes on her, she couldn't keep the Light from brightening her face. After standing up to princes and the greatest of humanity's warriors, it was galling to feel so exposed beneath this man's gaze.

"You may call me Serena," she said at last. It felt appropriate that he at least know her true name, if they were to plot treason together.

"You already know mine," he replied, a smile touching his lips. "I wish you the blessing of our gods below, Serena."

Then his image flickered and went out.

TWELVE

The rumble of voices around the gladiator complex was the loudest Hazel had ever heard it. She shouldn't be surprised. She and Johanas had made sure that the news the Alfur were planning a planetary cull had spread far and wide—and that the five cities should meet to discuss what they were going to do about it.

So they found themselves standing in the clearing near the forest's edge, the emerald sun dipping slowly towards the horizon behind them, waiting for the excitement to start.

Thankfully, most were still in the dark about Rydian's return. They intended to use that to their advantage.

Though Hazel couldn't help but think their entire plan was a long shot. Relying on the gladiators of other cities alone was a terrible risk. Relying on the word of an Alfur...

No, we are relying on Rydian, she reassured herself. *If*

all else fails, we still have him. For now, we take this one step at a time.

The first step was to get the other gladiators on board. Their help would be needed if they were to truly challenge the Alfur, but distrust between the cities had been seeded by generations of bloodshed. Not since the fall of Talamh had all the humans of their planet worked together. And that had ended in disaster.

It would take a miracle to unite them.

Hazel snorted to herself. Instead, they had Rydian Holt. She sent down a prayer to the gods that inhabited the planet's core that he could find a way to pull it off.

Thankfully, there were at least no Alfur in the complex today, and wouldn't be until the next games to take place in three weeks' time.

The same day, according to Rotin, that the planetary cull was to begin.

Somehow, news of that atrocity failed to touch Hazel. Sure, she feared for her people. But shock? How many times could one be shocked by the atrocities of the Alfur, before you stopped being surprised?

Standing in that open field, she made a promise to her gods, to go with her prayer. That she would not stop with Goma's liberation. Not even when all of Talamh breathed sweet freedom would she cease her campaign. After all they had done, the vile deeds committed in their names, the Alfur could not be allowed to continue.

And Hazel would make it her life's charge to exterminate every last member of the vile species.

Starting with Rotin, once they had what they needed from her.

She sucked in a sudden breath and forced her thoughts back to the present. The hulking presence of Johanas was comforting alongside her, but the sight of an agitated Falcon was more than enough to equalise her emotions. The Goman champion hadn't wanted any of this. Hazel wasn't surprised. Falcon had to be one of the most egocentric, selfish people she had ever known. What did it matter to a woman like Falcon if the world burned? So long as she had her bottle of spirits and someone to kill, she wouldn't complain.

With a curse, Hazel dismissed the woman from her mind. She didn't matter today. What mattered was the others, those who still had loved ones back in the cities, who cared for their adoring fans.

That was why they had gathered everyone here. Out in the open field, away from the buildings and their Light, there was no way of being overheard. Not even with some secret device secreted away in the walls. The trees and grass could be trusted with the secrets humanity would discuss this evening. Though...

...Hazel couldn't help but shiver as she glanced back at the trees. Darkness lay within. Only once had she entered those shadows, on the night they had lost Aureli. It wasn't a good memory, and she found herself retreating a step. Many of her fellow gladiators were casting similar glances at the trees. Rydian might be comfortable in those shadows, but wiser heads recalled the beasts that hid within.

Some spell or technology used by the Alfur had kept them from this place, but within the shadows, all bets were off.

She wondered how Rydian had survived so long inside, even with the Light.

The voices grew louder around Hazel as the gladiators began to jostle one another. No one had told them what to expect once they arrived here, only to come, and now they were growing impatient. She looked around for Rydian. He had better make his move shortly, or they would have other problems. Tensions were already high with news of the cull, and while each city was not *the* enemy responsible, they were *an* enemy.

She noted Falcon standing at the head of the Goman gladiators. Arms crossed and lips pursed, the Goman champion made no effort to calm the crowd—or even her own people. She swayed slightly in place, her eyes glassy cursed. The woman had gotten worse since Aureli's death, she was sure of it.

But that was a worry for another day.

Light appeared amongst the trees. The silence wasn't immediate, but rather spaced out as those nearest the shadows noticed the phenomenon and whispered to their friends. A hush fell slowly over their ranks as all eyes turned towards the jungle.

So it was that not a single eye failed to witness Rydian's arrival.

"Told you it would work," Johanas said.

"It hasn't worked yet," she reminded him gently.

She still wasn't convinced. Rydian hadn't exactly been

popular amongst the gladiators, even before word had gotten out that he was the son of *the* traitor. However, there was a certain madness to his plan that had its appeal. Or at least, a madness that might appeal to the particular type of souls that fought in the gladiator arenas of Talamh.

The crowd drew back as Rydian approached them, leaving a great open space in their centre. No wonder, he was quite the sight with the spotted cat at his side. Just the sight of the creature should have sent half their numbers fleeing, but the Light drew their attention, held them fixed in place, waiting with their questions, seeking their answers.

Rydian's hand was one thing, but today...today it was not just the artificial hand, but an entire blade of Light that lit the fading day. It blazed a pure white, glinting sharply in the emerald sunset.

Hazel's skin crawled at the sight of the weapon. She had tried to fight *that?* With an ordinary gladius? What else was Rydian capable of with that power burning inside of him?

Moments passed, and then new whispers began to spread. It didn't take long for Hazel to identify their source. Her fellow gladiators had recognised the strange man standing amongst them.

"People of Talamh!" His voice rung out suddenly over the whispers. "Do you know why I have come?"

Silence. A hundred eyes watched Rydian, but not one dared to speak. Not until...

"To put on a Light show, I hope!" Falcon called out

over the heads of the other gladiators. Her voice slurred as she continued. "Make some pretty pictures in the sky for us, Rydian."

Hazel winced and a frown crossed Rydian's face as he looked for Falcon amongst the crowd. But Falcon's jeer had broken the spell over the gathered gladiators, and other voices called out before he could speak again.

"Get outa here, traitor!"

"Go back to ya stinking Alfur!"

"*Enough!*" Rydian's voice rang across the clearing. His eyes burned as it swept the crowd. The silence was instant this time. "I am no traitor," he continued between clenched teeth. "And I have come to ask for your help. You know the news that passes between the barracks. The Alfur must be stopped. We're the only ones that can do it."

"Just rumours..."

"Bugger that..."

"...don't stand a chance."

The voices began again, until a burst of brilliant Light exploded from Rydian. It swept across the crowd, burning bright. Several warriors threw themselves on the ground in efforts to avoid it, but it didn't seem to cause any harm. Just a warning then.

"*I* am the proof," Rydian growled. "Proof that the Alfur have lied to us all these centuries. That we have been used, our true potential caged, so that we could not threaten them. But mistake me not, each and every one of us holds the power to match the Alfur. I will show you all."

Hazel pursed her lips as she listened to Rydian speak. This part had been a gamble. They still didn't have a solution to the Haze—though Hazel was willing to risk it, if it meant taking revenge upon the Alfur. But showing the others the Light could open the doors to anarchy and chaos.

There was silence for a while at that, as though the other gladiators were waiting for something, some sign that the man standing before them spoke the truth.

"Prove it," it was Falcon again who spoke. Her voice was clearer now. She pushed herself to the front of the crowd and stood before Rydian and the great cat.

Confronted by the woman, Rydian hesitated. "Prove what?"

"That the Alfur can be killed."

"You know they can," he said quietly. "You saw me, just before I faced Rotin. How could I be standing here now, if I had not defeated her?"

"So Rotin is dead?"

Beneath the eyes of his fellows, Rydian hesitated. "No," he said at last. "I spared her."

Murmurings spread through the crowd as Falcon shook her head. "So it's true," she snarled. "You're an Alfurian sympathiser. What is this then, some trap to lure us all to our doom?"

Hazel's heart was racing. What was Falcon doing? She had refused to help Rydian, sure, but this was far beyond that. Why would she sabotage their plans, destroy any hope they had of defeating the Alfur...?

Because she doesn't want to lose.

Clenching her teeth, Hazel pushed forward through the throng of gladiators until she stood beside Falcon.

"Coward," she spat, her voice carrying over the whisperings of the crowd. "Are you truly so fond of your own skin that you would see us all stand by while millions die?"

There was a glint to Falcon's eyes as she turned to face Hazel. "And what's it to you, Hawk?" she sneered. She made a gesture towards Rydian. "Did you not try to end our little Mouse here, the last time you met? Why don't you try it again now? We can all see this new power of his in action."

Hazel swallowed as she looked into the woman's eyes and saw the hatred there, the bitterness. "No," she said softly. She had already confronted that pain inside her, the agony that screamed for her to lash out, to strike down Rydian and anyone else connected to her brother's death. "I will leave my anger for the Alfur."

So saying, she turned from the woman and crossed the clearing to where Rydian stood. Laying a hand upon his shoulder, she turned to the watching gladiators. Falcon stared back.

"I trust Rydian Holt," Hazel said, loud enough that all who had gathered could hear. "If he says we can fight back against the Alfur, I believe him."

A whispering began in the crowd. She swallowed, knowing it was not enough. Not yet.

"You all know me by now," she continued. "Falcon was right. I was part of the resistance, along with my brother. I was there the day they fell. They killed everyone there. Everyone but me, because I was too young to meet their sick idea of justice. But I witnessed something that day. In the Alfur. Fear. They didn't want us finding what lay in their temple. Whatever was in there, it has been moved. But we will find it again, and use it against them."

She drew in a breath, but still the crowd was not moved. Hazel knew what they were waiting for, what they needed to hear. Could she speak the words out loud?

"Rydian's mother was no traitor," she said softly. "The Alfur lied, to destroy her reputation, and the reputation of the resistance."

Now the whispers began, the rumbling of words as men and women turned to one another in question. A new commotion came from the crowd as Johanas made his way forward.

"You know me as well." His rumbling voice carried over the clearing. "I have bandaged many of your wounds, whichever city you hail from. Hear me now, the time of division must end. We cannot continue, city against city. It is time humanity united against our true enemy. Against the ones who send unwilling men and women to die on their bloody sands. Against those who would commit casual genocide on our people. We must fight the Alfur, not ourselves."

Silence. Not a soul spoke as the gladiators or Talamh stood at the edge of the wilderness and stared at the man that had come to liberate them. Hazel swallowed. Had they said enough, done enough, to swing things towards them. Or had she failed again, like every other time she had tried...

"Fine," it was Falcon who spoke. She lifted her chin to stare at them. "Once, Marcus Aureli bid me join him in a rebellion against the Alfur. I rebuked him that day. I have always regretted it. If there is a war to be had, let it not be said Falcon of Goma stood by and did nothing."

Hazel stared at the woman, shocked by her words. How...they couldn't possibly...this...unless...

Her eyes narrowed as she turned to look at Rydian. Her friend kept his eyes carefully averted though, watching the crowd. She cursed beneath her breath. Had all that with Falcon been a setup?

If so, it had worked. Already others were nodding, rumbling their approval. Swords were drawn and raised towards the setting sun. Vows were sworn. And one by one, the gladiators of the five cities swore to defend their people from the cull.

Whatever it took.

THIRTEEN

Three days passed, and still Serena was no closer to the truth her father had hidden from her. She was practically bouncing from the walls of her chambers with the frustration of it all. Honestly, how did the humans do it? Lie to one another like this, withhold truths. Lock each other away. Better to be sent to the arena without even a weapon to defend herself than this, surely.

And yet it continued.

No one came. Even the other heirs stopped their checking in. She supposed even her most steadfast ally in Cassia must grow wary of Serena's endless pestering eventually.

The guards certainly never check in on her.

Serena was isolated, cut off from her people in a way she had never been before. It was galling, terrifying, soul crushing.

It also gave her a chance to truly view the actions of

her people from an outside perspective. From the view of someone like Rydian, who had spent his entire life living beneath Alfurian reign.

She didn't like what she saw.

She had thought she'd known their pain, but living in isolation, locked away unjustly as so many humans had been, she found she hadn't begun to understand. Still couldn't, really. What would it be like to be one of the unsuspecting humans selected for the cull? To have tried all their lives to go unnoticed, to prosper in a world outside their control, only to find their overlords had decided their time on Talamh had come to an end.

Several times she tried to contact her father. But he remained steadfast in his determination to ignore her. Nothing she did seemed to matter. She even tried cutting her rations of Light off altogether. Refusing the sustenance had left her drained and ill. Surely this must bring him, she had thought, even as her skin turned a paled grey, the Light beneath dimming with each passing hour.

But still he had not come, and the next day Serena had known she must take her rations, or risk far graver illness. Obviously, her father's resolve was stronger than her own.

It took those three days for Serena to realise she'd been going about things the wrong way. She was protesting her confinement as an Alfur might. With strong words and persistent calls and personal confrontation.

But acting like an Alfur would not get her father's attention. It never had.

Only one thing could drag her father away from his duties.

It was time Serena Levaanton started acting like a human.

Her bed was made of a steel frame fixed together by brackets to support the down mattress. Solid enough—if all you were doing was sleeping on it.

If you were deliberately trying to dismantle the thing, however...

She had resumed her regimen of Light the night before. Her strength renewed, it took only a few kicks to tear the metal headboard from the base. The heavy steel slammed to the ground with a ringing crash. She stood over it a moment, watching the doorway, but apparently the commotion wasn't yet enough to attract her guards.

No matter. There was plenty more she could break.

In the end, it took another ten minutes and the wonton destruction of half her furniture before the sounds finally gained the attention of her keepers.

Serena paused as the doors to her chambers opened with a hiss. She was partway through dismantling her sofa. One of the poles from her bed had made a fine club, helping to break the legs and inner structure down into more manageable pieces. It was half raised for the next blow as the guards stepped through the doorway.

Both the guards and Serena froze. A long moment passed as their gazes passed over the room. Her bed was in a dozen pieces by then, as was the sofa. It was a shame, really, to see such a magnificent piece of furniture brought low. The velvet had come all the way from Lutryde, on the other side of the planet, while the wooden frame would have been made from wood fallen naturally in the forests around Goma—a painstaking process, even with an Alfurian vessel available for transport.

Now it lay in ruins, all that hard work, come to nothing...

...it was odd though, it had felt strangely curative, all this wanton destruction. Perhaps that explained the humans' rioting.

No matter. For the moment, Serena had what she wanted, the faces of her captors brightened with their shock.

"Princess!" The first exclaimed.

"What happened?" The other cried.

Serena blinked, looking from her destruction to the pair. Apparently, these two couldn't quite process the fact *she* had caused all the damage. She supposed it made sense. Afterall, no Alfur in the history of Talamh had behaved as such. Well, if they needed more of a demonstration...she was happy to oblige. Apparently.

Grinning, she raised her bar and smashed the eating table in a single blow, then turned to them again.

"Why, I only thought to send father a message," she said, flashing her lashes in a very human manner. "But I couldn't seem to reach him."

The faces of her guards grew brighter still. They exchanged a look—then fled from her chambers.

Serena took a seat amidst the rubble as the doors hissed closed, smiling to herself.

This time, she didn't have to wait long for her father's arrival.

He arrived in a swirling of silk robes, his face like a thundercloud, a curse on his lips.

"Why father," she said, rising, "I see you got my message."

"Your...what...message..." he spluttered, eyes darting about his face as he took in her room. "*What were you thinking?*"

Serena felt another wave of satisfaction wash over her. It soothed her turmoiled soul to see her father so distressed. After so much time in isolation, she had begun to feel as though he truly controlled everything, that his plans, the councils plans, could not be stopped.

His distress standing amidst the wreckage caused by his own daughter was proof Aiden Levaanton could be outmanoeuvred. She just had to think outside the box her people had been placed inside.

"I figured since you were so intent on treating me like a human, I may as well act like one."

Her father's mouth opened and closed, but no words came out. It was several moments before he seemed to pull his wits about himself.

"Serena, this is most unbecoming."

"I suppose it is," she mused. Crossing to her dining table—which was about the only piece of furniture that remained intact, she took a seat.

Her father stood for a moment watching her, then exhaled. "Very well," he hissed. "What is it you wanted, Daughter?"

"My freedom," she replied, reclining in her chair. "Or failing that, answers."

"Can I trust you not to interfere with council business if I grant you the halls?"

"Most likely not," she replied matter-of-factly. She might be inclined to misbehave, but she was Alfur still, and lying was not in their nature.

"Then no."

"I suppose it must be answers then."

Her father passed a wary hand across his face. "Answers require questions."

"By all means, Father. Take a seat, and I will ask them."

He sighed, and it seemed for a hearts beat that he would walk away. But the past weeks must have tired him more than she knew, for at last he crossed to her table and slumped into the opposite seat, defeated.

"Why do we fear the humans so?" she whispered. "And don't give the same tiresome explication about their Light. If we needed too, our ships could annihilate their population with hardly an effort."

"Is that what you think?" her father said softly.

"I thought I was the one asking the questions."

He said nothing for a time, only watched her, as though waiting for Serena to say more.

She obliged.

"I know about the installation the rebellion attacked," she said. As she spoke, she watched her father for a reaction, for some sign of the secrets he kept. "That we had Alfur stationed there, even before the humans attacked." She shook her head, a curse on her lips as still her father did not speak. "What I cannot understand though, is what could possibly be so important on the planet's surface?"

"I think you are mistaken, Daughter."

"You know that I am not."

Silence fell as father and daughter stared across the table at one another, each unblinking, unwilling to back down. A tremor shook Serena, but she was firm now, determined to get to the bottom of this entire mystery. If there really was a weapon the humans could use—

"Very well, Daughter," he said suddenly. "If you must know, it is not the humans that we fear. It is their effect on the Haze that concerns us."

"The Haze..." she trailed off, a frown creasing her features.

"Yes," her father confirmed. "There is a link between it and the animals of this planet. As you know, it drives them insane once they hit puberty. But recently, we have begun to observe another phenomenon. Surges in the Haze. It seems they relate to the collective emotion of the humans in the general area. In Goma. That was what our station was monitoring—trying to identify the exact makeup of the connection. So that we might thwart it."

"Why would we need to thwart it? The Haze does not

affect us. And the humans are protected, so long as they wear their Manus readers"

"For now." Aiden Levaanton drew in a breath. "The truth is, we know dangerously little about the phenomenon ..." He trailed off with a shake of his head.

Serena pursed her lips. "So why was the council so panicked when the humans broke into this 'monitoring room' of yours? Why did you tell us all it was a weapons storage facility for the Enforcers?" She leaned forward across the table. "Why did you *lie* to me, Father?"

He sighed. "Because..." His eyes flickered closed, the Light beneath his skin flickering, dimming. "Because I have not told you everything." He looked up suddenly, their eyes meeting once more. "It is not just a monitoring facility, Serena. We are still experimenting with the Haze, trying to find a way through, to connect with...with the rest of our peoples."

The breath caught in Serena's throat and her hearts grew still. "What?"

"We seek to reconnect with the outside universe, Serena."

Serena could only stare. That was the greatest secret of the Alfur, one not even she would reveal to the humans. That they could not leave this planet. That the insidious tendrils of the Haze had trapped them on the surface for a thousand years, interfering with any Alfurian ship that left the atmosphere. Even their communications had been cut off, unable to pass through the aura that surrounded the planet. Serena and all those of her generation had never set eyes on their home world, never even talked to another soul from the galaxies beyond Talamh.

"You thought the humans might destroy your work," she whispered.

"Or use it," he muttered, then shook himself. "Yes. The technology does not work up here. It must be kept close to the planet's surface, to avoid being corrupted by the Haze itself. That is why we kept this...installation close, hidden within the human city. We did not expect the revolutionaries to discover its importance."

"I see..." Serena mused, her mind working quickly. It did not sound as though this installation was the weapon the humans had hoped for, but perhaps it might still have its uses. If they could find it again. "But...that means it must still be inside the city?"

"No," her father replied. "We extended the lower levels of our tower. A great expense of Light was used, but it was a necessary cost, after how close they came..." He shivered. "Truly, if the woman Jasmine had not experienced a crisis of conscience, we could have lost everything. It is well guarded now."

Serena hardly heard his last words. Her hearts were racing again, already imagining escaping from this room and journeying deep into the depths of this tower, to where the secrets of the Haze waited to be exposed. If they were truly so close to piercing its mists, maybe, just maybe, she could contact those on the outside. After everything her father and the council had done, surely they must condemn the princes, must come and aid Serena in her quest to protect the humans.

And if not...well, maybe Rydian and his friends could use the installation as a bargaining chip, a way to prevent the genocide of their people.

It was a small hope, but after weeks in isolation, Serena would take it.

FOURTEEN

"THAT WAS SOME PERFORMANCE, FALCON," JOHANAS announced as he stepped into Aureli's old chambers.

Sitting wearily at the table alongside Hazel and Falcon, Rydian offered his friend a weak smile. "Almost too good," he admitted. "If Hazel hadn't stepped up..."

"Ah but we knew she would!" Johanas exclaimed. Crossing the room, he swept the woman up into a hug.

She scowled at him, but gave his back a pat anyway before they drew apart. "A little warning would have been nice," she said archly, flashing them all a glare.

Rydian's cheeks grew warm, but Falcon only cackled. "You're a terrible actress, my dear," she replied. "If you wanted them to support this insane plan of yours—and it is insane—then you could hardly rely on the son of a known traitor. And only your word would do to clear Rydian of his mother's dark mark."

Hazel's face darkened, and Rydian knew she was

remembering that fateful night when his mother had betrayed everything the rebellion had stood for.

"I believe you, Hazel," he said into the silence. Her head whipped around at his words, her brown eyes widening. He swallowed. He'd meant to do this privately, but... well, this needed to be said. "I believe my mother betrayed the resistance. I don't know why. Maybe something in that room affected her. Maybe something destroyed her Manus reader, exposed her to the Haze." He exhaled, and struggled to hold Hazel's gaze. "We may never know. But I accept it happened. That she turned against you. That she killed your brother. That she betrayed us all."

Hazel said nothing for the longest of moments. Finally, she gave a little nod. "Thank you." The words came out as the barest of whispers.

A longer silence followed, until at last Falcon snorted. "Well, now that that is sorted." She stood, looking around the room. "I will leave you to your schemes." She turned to go.

"Falcon," Rydian spoke before he could second guess himself. The woman froze. "What you said back there? Did you really mean it?"

Falcon turned slowly, her sapphire eyes looking from Rydian to Hazel to Johanas. He noticed her clench her fist, and glimpsed the Light there.

"I wish I could help you," she said at last. The Light brightened for a moment, then died out. "But I cannot use the Light any longer." She laughed, though the sound was without any trace of humour. "We thought it such a miracle, when we made the discovery. Thought we could handle the pain that came with it, with all the power it gave us. We were wrong."

"You're at the edge," Rydian said.

Falcon nodded. Her eyes fell to her Manus reader. "This device is the only thing that keeps me sane now. So you see..." she swallowed. "I cannot help you. Not with this fight."

"But you can," Johanas said gently. "We don't need more fighters, Falcon. We have a whole complex of those. We need your knowledge. To learn how to deactivate the devices, how to hide it from the Alfur."

"Your friend in her gilded tower will know," Falcon said matter-of-factly.

Hazel snorted. "Like I'd trust one of *them* with something that important. No, we can't all go cutting off our hands like Rydian here."

"*I* didn't cut it off."

"I'm sure."

"Come and join us for a drink, Falcon," Johanas urged, ignoring the pair of them. "We can discuss business later."

Falcon laughed at that. "Well, let it not be said that Falcon ever turned down an offer for free booze." She paused, eying the empty table. "Though so far the offerings seem terribly sparse."

"Ahh..." Johanas trailed off, looking to the others in askance.

Rydian laughed. Thankfully, he'd seen where Falcon had stashed her supply the last night they'd sat there. He rose and he crossed to the pantry, where he fished out several bottles and glasses from the secret compartment. Falcon watched him as he returned, prize in hand. One eyebrow arched high on her forehead.

"Bribing me with my own spirits, are we?"

Grinning, Rydian shook his head. "Let's think of it more as your first contribution towards our shared endeavour."

The woman rolled her eyes at that, but she accepted the glass he passed her. Once he'd ensured everyone had one of their own, Rydian met the eyes of each of his companions, and raised his glass.

"To the future," he said, voice solemn.

"To the future," the others repeated.

To a future for all, Fatimah's voice tickled his mind, as a rumble came from the corner where the big cat had curled itself into a ball.

The surprise on the faces of his friend told Rydian the cat had spoken to all of them. He grinned. "See, Falcon, even the cat believes in our plan."

The bird warrior is right, Fatimah interjected before the others could reply. *It is madness. But what is life without a little risk?*

Falcon chuckled at that. "Thank you, great one," she said, inclining her head towards the beast.

"Yes, well, if you don't all mind, how about we drink to our future already?"

Several hours later, Hazel lay slumped across the table and even Johanas had curled up in the corner, both passed out cold, the only signs of life was the rumbling of the giant's snoring, and the occasional grunt from Hazel.

Rydian had been somewhat surprised to find the alcohol did not affect him like it had before. Something about the Light, he supposed. Even as he finished yet another glass, the fiery liquid burning right until it reached his stomach, still he felt only a pleasant buzz at the back of his mind.

And Falcon, of course, remained her usual drunk but decidedly conscious self.

"So what made you change your mind?" Rydian asked as he poured himself another drink.

"Would you believe me if I said it was your inspiring speech?"

Rydian snorted. "I don't think I even convinced myself."

Falcon nodded along with his words. "So what makes you think my mind has really changed?"

Staring her in the eyes, Rydian felt a sudden doubt in his heart, that perhaps he'd been wrong. That the change of heart that had come over Falcon had only been an act. The woman said nothing though, only sipped from her glass and watched the sleeping pair. Johanas, with all his strength. Hazel, with all her pain.

"I was all convinced to let you burn out," she said at last. "I've seen this happen to others, through the years. Their Manus reader malfunctions and suddenly their faster, stronger. Most use it to find success in the arena." She blinked, looking from their friends to Rydian. "But not you. You could have beaten her easily, killed her for what happened in the arena. But you didn't," she sighed. "I guess I'll owe the old man a drink, when we meet in the underworld. He always said you were different."

"Aureli?"

Falcon didn't seem to hear him. "All these years in the arena, all these years with the Haze, with the Light and the *burning*...I guess I forgot there was another world. One without pain. One where humanity could work together."

Rydian swallowed. "I hope so," he said softly, his eyes drifting away. They sat in darkness but for his glowing hand. "But I find myself doubting sometimes as well."

"Obviously," Falcon said wryly. "Only a madman wouldn't doubt a plan that pitches a bunch of ragtag gladiators against the might of the Alfur." She paused. "Which, admittedly, fits the company."

Rydian snorted into his drink. "So do you really think this will work?"

"That depends."

"On what?"

A grin spread across Falcon's face. "On whether you want me to lie to you or not?"

Rydian couldn't help but laugh at that. But he didn't need the drunken gladiator's faith, only her support. Before he could reply, however, a tingling spread through his artificial hand, like a soft buzzing, almost like...

He jumped as a hologram sprang to life on the table between them. A curse slipped from Falcon's lips. The old gladiator was on her feet before Rydian could even summon his Light blade. His fist was half clenched, preparing to arm himself, before he realised what was happening.

The hologram standing on the table between them was of Rotin—or Serena, as she had told him to call her. This time, thankfully, she was fully clothed. The look on her face as she stared at him, however, immediately put his nerve on high alert.

"Rydian Holt," she said formally, her voice ringing softly in the almost bare chambers. "Are you alone?"

He shared a glance with Falcon, who's eyes were still wide. Her blade had stopped halfway from its sheath.

"Not quite."

The hologram rotated. He wasn't sure exactly how the technology—or was it magic in this case—worked, but apparently she could now see his company.

"Falcon," she greeted. "So you're in the gladiator complex. That...complicates things."

"Oh don't worry, Alfur, that's not our only complication," Falcon said, her voice dangerous. Her eyes turned on Rydian. "What is one of *them* doing, contacting you?"

Shaking himself, Rydian finally managed to gather his wits. "She's on our side," he said, then narrowed his eyes. "I think."

"I am," Serena said firmly.

His heart quickened. "Then you have the information we need?"

Silence followed. The silence, Rydian thought, of someone perhaps having second thoughts. He swallowed.

If Serena decided to betray them, their rebellion was doomed before it began.

But then, they were doomed without her information anyway, weren't they?

"I have...something."

"What is it?"

"The place your mother and her rebels attacked, you were right. There were Alfur operating there. It was important to my people."

"Important how?" Rydian asked quicky.

Another pause. "I'm...still not sure about that. Important enough that my father and the council lied to the rest of the Alfur about it. That is no minor thing, amongst my people."

"Thank the Gods below," Rydian murmured, then paused. He still sensed a hesitation about Serena's responses. "What aren't you telling us, Serena?"

A sigh came from the hologram. "Whatever was in the facility, it is no longer in Goma," she said quietly. "At least, not the human part. My father had it moved to our family tower."

Rydian's heart plummeted into his stomach. Just today, a message from the Alfur had confirmed the next games would finally be held again in Goma. Their plan had been to sneak aboard one of the ships ferrying gladiators into the city, then seek out this secret facility of the Alfur. But if it had been moved into the Alfurian towers...

"I'm liking our odds considerably less," Falcon muttered. "Why are we working with this creature again?"

Rydian sighed. "For information like this."

"The room will be under heavy guard," Serena added, as though the facility being located in one of the Alfurian towers wasn't enough. "They will destroy whatever they're guarding if any of you come close to the facility."

"Then what do we do?" Rydian asked, his shoulders slumping.

"I have a plan," the Alfur said quietly. "Only...you're going to need to break me out of house arrest first."

FIFTEEN

IT HAD PHYSICALLY HURT FOR HAZEL TO SPEAK THOSE lies in front of all the gladiators of Talamh. But Rydian's admission, his acceptance of what his mother had done, had been an impossible dream come true. His denial, how he had avoided the subject of his mother, of her dead brother, had been a dagger in the side of their friendship. Now it was gone. Whatever the world beyond the three friends believed, they three knew the truth.

It was enough.

After the last year of her life, it was more than she could have hoped.

How things had changed in a few short months. Before her brother's death, she had dared hope for normal things. To grow up, live a life with as little interference by the Alfur as possible. To one day fall in love with a fellow human.

Who would have thought she would end up killing

them instead? That in a matter of days, she would raise her blade against their Alfurian overlords.

All because of one woman. The mother of the man that would stand alongside her. So many times now, she had replayed that terrible night in her mind, the moment when Jasmine Holt plunged the sword through her brother's back. The pain in Solomon's eyes as he'd died.

That had been the moment Hazel's childhood had died. Her innocence had been burned away in the subsequent slaughter, until all that had remained was the cold hatred, the fiery anger of her promise. That one day she would have her revenge.

An impossible task, to go against the Alfur. Yet here amongst the gladiator's of Talamh, twice she had seen it happen. Once, as Johanas had stood in open defiance of their decree, had refused their orders to kill. The giant gladiator had been willing to put his life on the line for his convictions. Hazel could do no less. But first, she had needed to fight this war of hers.

Rydian had shown her that path. Shown her with his defiance of Rotin. With his very survival. She didn't believe for a moment they had spared him for sparing the prince's daughter. For all his power, Rydian was still a naïve young man. He couldn't see the truth. That the prince hadn't dared act against him. That Aiden Levaanton, overlord of all the humans in Goma, had been afraid.

Hazel would not make the same mistake.

Sitting in the airship, Hazel stared at the device embedded in the palm of her hand. Her memories of her youth, before it had been implanted, before her family had...perished, were faint. It had been a part of her for almost as long as she could remember.

She clenched her fist. A part of her. But not on her side. It was another traitor. A treacherous reminder of the control the Alfur had exercised over Hazel all her life.

Today, for better or worse, that control would end.

"Are you sure about this?" Falcon asked.

The senior gladiator sat on the bench across from Hazel. Her worn face wore an expression of concern. Hazel might have been touched, if she didn't still possess an intense dislike for this woman. Falcon had stood by while a generation of young Goman gladiators had been slaughtered. Her negligence had almost gotten Hazel and her friends killed in their first bout—would have, most likely, had it not been for Aureli.

Now she had finally decided to help them...it hardly seemed enough now, at the final hour.

"Of course," Hazel said, her voice hard. "I am no coward."

"It is not cowardice to fear for your own sanity."

Hazel pursed her lips. She did her best to ignore the voices that whispered in her mind as she held out her hand to falcon. Forehead still creased in a frown, she accepted Hazel's palm. A scalpel balanced between her fingers. Hazel winced as the razor point touched her flesh, and looked away.

Falcon was right, of course. She did fear what came next. How could she not, after what had become of

Aureli? And Falcon, for that matter. She couldn't believe the drunken, bitter woman they had first met on the field of the gladiator complex had once partnered with Aureli.

And then of course there was Rydian. He hid it well, but she could see the pain in his face at times, when he thought no one was watching. Even the great cat, Fatimah, had seemed on edge the past few days. It was clear whatever they had done to stave off the dangers of the Haze, its effects were already wearing off.

The more you use the Light, the greater its influence over you.

That was what Falcon had said to them, before they had decided on their course. But there was no other option. Rydian could not fight all the Alfur of Goma alone, even if they *did* fear him. He needed backup. And whatever their progress as warriors, his fellow gladiators would not be enough. Even a human Enforcer equipped with Alfurian weaponry would be too much for them.

They needed more.

They needed the Light.

Hazel winced as she felt another pinching from her palm. Falcon raised her head, which was barely a few inches from Hazel's Manus reader, and scowled.

"Would you hold still?" she snapped. "This is a very delicate procedure."

Hazel glowered back at the woman. That was the Falcon she knew. She said nothing though, only looked around, catching the eyes of her friends nearby. Rydian only raised an eyebrow.

"Chicken," he teased. "You'd think she was cutting off your hand or something."

Snorting despite herself, Hazel shook her head. "We aren't all so dedicated to the cause."

Rydian laughed despite being the object of her jest. Seated on the bench alongside him, Johanas only grunted.

He was next.

"What if you're wrong?" she asked suddenly, her eyes meeting Rydian's blue eyes.

The words had left Hazel before she could hold them back. She knew why she'd said them though. They were here because of him, after all. Because he had dared to hope in the Light, where others like Falcon had seen only the doom of the Haze.

A frown creased Rydian's face. He paused, as though carefully considering her words. A smile touched his lips.

"Then we die."

Hazel's mouth was already open, a follow up question on her tongue, but it died on her lips. Silence fell across the ship. It was a moment before she realised Rydian's words had been heard not just by the three of them, but by all the Goman gladiators aboard.

She swallowed. It wasn't like she hadn't *known* that was their likely fate here. Every man and woman onboard probably guessed as much. But to hear it out loud...

Somewhere, a man coughed. The spell broke and men and women turned back to one another. Conversation slowly returned. When Hazel was satisfied the others had returned to minding their own business, she leaned closer to Rydian.

"Damnit, Rydian. Were you in that jungle a few months, or born in it?"

He chuckled. "You did ask."

"No one wants that much honesty."

"We're all going to die, Hazel," he said, thankfully quieter than before. Sitting back on the bench, he looked from her to Johanas. "That's the truth, what you realised that day in the arena, wasn't it, Johanas?"

The former gladiator frowned, but gave the slightest nod of his head. Rydian smiled and continued in a louder voice, drawing attention back to them.

"I meant what I said. We are gladiators. That means we face death every week. We all knew it back in the barracks, whether we admitted it out loud or not. That death stalks us. That one day soon we would lie in the earth with our Gods. We have all felt that despair."

Silence returned to the ship now. Hazel wanted to curse Rydian for destroying their morale, but there was no stopping him now.

"That despair, that is the despair of every slave, of every soul on Talamh. To know your destiny is not your own. Our mentor, Marcus Aureli, he told me once that he had found a freedom in the arena, in the knowledge that on the sands his life was finally his own." Rydian shook his head. "He was wrong. His death was in his hands, but not his life. Not the reason he fought."

"Today, that changes. Today, we might all die, or only

a few. It will not come without cost. Freedom never does. But know that if you fall today, it will not be for the amusement of the mob, or the cruel whims of the Alfur. It will be because you had the courage to stand and fight for something worthwhile. Today the men and women of Talamh fight not for a name, or a sword, or glory, but the fate of their peoples. Of the human race itself." He smiled. "That, my friends, is a cause worth dying for."

Not a soul spoke as Rydian fell silent, but he held the attention of every soul aboard the ship. Finally he turned his back to them and sat. A self-deprecating smile touched his lips as he looked around his circle of friends.

"Too much?"

Falcon rolled her eyes. "You think?"

Hazel didn't speak for a long moment. "I hope you're right, Rydian."

He smiled back at her. "Me too."

SIXTEEN

Johanas *burned*.

Rydian had described the sensation to them before they had taken the decision to ascend. But hearing about the Haze was one thing. Experiencing it was...something altogether less pleasant.

Hazel had screamed when Falcon deactivated her Manus reader in the airship. Johanas didn't remember what he had done. Rydian told him he had screamed...but truth be told, his memories were all scarlet agony, his actions burned way by the fiery Light. That pain...his veins had felt like molten metal, like the fabric of his soul was tearing from the power inside him.

At first though, it had seemed just a tiny spark within, a dwindling, depleted thing. As though a part of it had been sucked away by the trappings of the Manus reader. He sensed the Alfur had been taking something from them all these years, that the Manus readers did not control their Light by suppressing it, but rather siphoning it off.

But such introspection was lost when the power had swelled. Its limits removed, that Light had expanded to fill his core, to consume every part of him in its flames, to turn his world to all-consuming energy. Sounds shrieked in his ears, sounds like the screams of a thousand voices, though surely that was only his imagination, only his own pain reflected back thousand-fold.

Pain, and rage like nothing Johanas had ever experienced.

His father had told Johanas the stories of their ancestors. Of strong men who had used their size and strength to resist. To conquer their neighbours. To forge a place for themselves in this violent world with violence of their own. All of them had died terrible, early deaths.

But Johanas, like his father before him, had decided to take the path of peace. To be a healer, rather than a killer.

Until the Alfur had taken him, and set him on a different path.

That first day in the gladiator complex, Johanas had known rage. A terrible anger at the injustice of this world. Maybe that was why he had succumbed to their demands, why he had been so weak. Why he'd killed others for their entertainment. Because of that rage, of the need to do something *anything*, to sate that terrible anger.

But it hadn't helped. Instead, each victory had left him empty inside. Bereft of purpose. His entire meaning in life, destroyed in a few instants of insanity.

Maybe Rydian was right, and that had been because there had been nothing to fight for then, that no matter how many gladiators battled and fought and died on the sands, there could be no hope for a true victory. No hope that they could achieve the victory they so desperately desired. The best they could hope for on the sands was a delay, a stay on their execution.

Until today.

Or so he hoped.

For today, Bloodlust would return to the sands of Goma. And Johanas would kill again.

Stepping from the shadows, he exhaled. A warm breeze blew through the arena, carrying with it the taste of dust and sweat. The emerald sun beat down high overhead, and a thousand souls stood in the stands, looking down into the centre of the arena in expectation. The Enforcers had gathered in greater numbers than normal. They stood in a ring around the sands, Light sticks held at the ready—though most had eyes only for the crowd.

The rumble of voices grew louder at Johanas's appearance. Months had passed in Goma without a single game. No gladiator knew what to expect here, the state in which they might find the city.

Unfortunately for Goma, Johanas's entrance wasn't likely to improve their disposition.

But then, he wasn't trying to.

A roar carried around the stands as he strode across the sands. The roar of a name that was not his own, of another gladiator who's place Johanas had taken. At first, the crowd didn't seem to notice the switch. Though as Johanas strode towards the barrier of Light, a hush came over parts of the stadium. It was no surprise. Despite the helmet that covered his face, Johanas—or Bloodlust as these people knew him—was unmistakeable with his bulk.

And after his stunt on their last visit to the city, Goma was no fan of his.

The hush quickly devolved into screams and jeering, as thousands hurled down curses upon his head. Faces contorted as men and women rose from their seats in outrage. Fists were waved and a thousand feet pounded the wooden stands. The people of Goma had not spent weeks upon weeks without a games, only for a coward to ruin the exhibition.

Johanas ignored them. What was their anger but a candle in the wind compared to his own? To the bonfire that raged within, fed by all the cruelties of this world, the pain his father had suffered, the agony of his own decisions.

What was any of this, beside the inferno of the Haze?

He strode across the shining sands and came to a stop before the barrier of the Light that split the stadium in two. Fists clenched, iron blade held in a vicelike grip, he looked through the barrier to where his supposed opponent stood. The gladiator was a Mayenken woman. She nodded a greeting at his arrival, and Johanas shivered as old instincts screamed from the back of his mind, enhanced by the trappings of the Haze.

Kill her kill her kill her.

He drew in a breath. No, today the gladiators of Talamh would not pit their blades upon one another. That was not the show they had planned for his fellow Gomans. As he met the woman's eyes, she gave the slightest incline of her head.

Around the stadium, the jeering of the crowd had died a little, as a thousand eyes looked to the Enforcers that controlled the games. The men and women who served the Alfurian interests were conversing on their platform above the sands. Johanas had no doubt as to the subject of their conversation.

The drums took longer to sound than usual, but begin they did. Judging by the mood of the crowd, the Enforcers could not afford to delay the show while they figured out what was happening. Rydian and Hazel had been counting on that. He swallowed as he glanced back at the stairwell leading down to the gladiator rooms.

Good luck, my friends.

An uneasy stillness came over the crowd as the pounding drums grew louder. The people of Goma held their collective breaths, all eyes fixed on the two warriors in the centre of the stadium. Would Bloodlust redeem himself after his previous crimes, and strike down the cursed Mayenken gladiator? Or would Goma again be shamed by his cowardice?

Neither, Johanas thought to himself as the drums grew louder.

Beyond the barrier, the Mayenken woman drew her blade. this Johanas hoped she didn't plan to betray him.

He had no desire to spill gladiator blood this day. His soul was already stained enough, without adding another innocent to his ledger.

With a final boom, the drums reached their crescendo.

Silence fell.

The Light barrier flashed out.

In the sudden stillness, Johanas and his fellow gladiator turned to the crowd. Light flashed, leaping from their skin, burning from their veins, spreading, filling, consuming as it worked its magic. Johanas gasped and almost fell at the power of it, but he had a job to do, a task he could not fail.

"People of Goma!" Johanas cried, and the Mayenken woman cried out with him. The Light burned from them, catching their words and amplifying them throughout the stadium. "Today, the resistance rises! Today, the Alfur fall!"

Stunned faces stared down into the arena, shocked by what the pair had just said. But the calls to the crowd were only the beginning. Johanas had come here for a reason.

With the Mayenken woman at his side, they turned towards the Enforcers guarding the sands of the arena.

And the bloodshed began.

SEVENTEEN

Waiting in the shadows for Johanas's signal, Rydian wondered if he would ever develop the patience of a man like Aureli. Their mentor had lived his entire life beneath the yolk of the Alfur. For years he had existed with the fires of the Haze, the burning of the Light within. In all that time, he had not acted on the innate desires of those forces. To lash out, to destroy, to burn his enemies to the ground.

Even with Fatimah beside him, he could sense that pounding now, the rhythmic banging of the drums against his mind. It only seemed to have grown louder since reaching the city. Almost as though something about the Haze responded to the gathering of all these people, to the surging emotion of the stadium above.

Rydian hoped not, or what came next would be like poking a raging leopard.

No offence, he added as he felt a rumbling from the great cat at his side.

The cat said nothing. It could feel the pounding as well. Recalling the state they'd each been in before the connection, Rydian shuddered at what would come should their bond fail. They had used a lot of Light to reach the gladiator complex, and they would use more yet before the day was done. When the Haze returned, it would sweep away their sanity like rooftiles before a raging storm.

So the waiting, the lingering in the shadows, had them each practically jumping out of their skins in anticipation. But they couldn't act yet. Not until Johanas had begun. Until the eyes of their Alfurian overlords were occupied elsewhere.

He wondered how Johanas and the other gladiators were handling their own experiences with the Light. His friend had been tense before they'd separated in the corridors beneath the arena. He hoped it was only nerves, and not second thoughts about what was to come. They couldn't afford doubts now. It was too late to go back. Johanas would already be stepping out onto the sands of the arena, while Rydian, Fatimah and Hazel...

...they waited outside the hanger where the Alfurian ships were kept during the games.

"We should go now," Hazel interrupted his thoughts, her voice a low hiss, "before someone discovers us."

Rydian frowned at his friend. He could see the Light burning in her eyes, and her skin had a soft glow in the gloom of the corridors. Was this the eager excitement of the Light speaking, or his friend's natural ferocity? It was difficult to say, but he shook his head anyway.

"Not yet," he replied, "not until we know they're distracted."

If they attacked before time, they risked the Alfur figuring out their true intentions, and sending their forces against Hazel and Rydian, rather than the gladiator uprising...

...well, what he hoped would be the gladiator uprising. Despite assurances from each of the city champions, he was by no means certain of their true loyalties. He could only hope each man and woman played their part this day.

Boom.

Rydian stumbled as the world shook. Dust tricked down from the stone ceilings. A roar echoed through the tunnel, as of a thousand voices raised as one. He and Hazel shared a glance.

Then faced the wrought iron doors as one.

Light bloomed in Rydian's artificial hand, burning, scorching, gathering strength. At his side, Fatimah growled, the sound low in its chest, a primal, feral sound that would set even the boldest of souls to trembling.

Boom.

This time, the sound came not from above, but the doors barring their path as they were blasted from their hinges. Cries of shock and pain echoed from within. An acrid smoke filled the corridor as ferrous iron caught light in the absolute heat of Rydian's Light blast.

He and Hazel and Fatimah strode through the dark smoke, into chaos.

The hanger was a broad, open area opening out beneath the eastern section of the arena. They had been here many times, but only ever to be sheparded to and from the waiting rooms beneath the stadium. But they had spent enough time here to know the layout—and its defences. Or lack of them, rather.

A dozen Enforcers were always stationed within the hanger, but this was territory far from the public. Other than the occasional unruly gladiator, they had little reason to concern themselves with things like keeping watch. Afterall, who would have the nerve to attack a location where the Alfur kept their ships. The things were literal machines of death, equipped with devices that made Manus readers look like a child's toy.

So it was then that the dozen Enforcers stationed within the hanger looked on with a mixture of shock and terror as Rydian and Hazel blasted their way inside. Thankful the Alfur rarely bothered themselves with such mundane matters as guarding their deadly ships, Rydian had downed two Enforcers with blasts of Light before they even began to react.

Energy crackled as the remaining Enforcers activated their energy batons. Powered by Light, they were capable of delivering a potentially fatal blow to any human that crossed them. To a human population armed with little more than rusted swords and spears, the weapons were a terrifying threat. Especially since each baton was attuned to their Enforcer's Manus reader—meaning they couldn't be turned against their wielder.

But with the Light thrumming in his veins, Rydian had little fear of the Enforcer's weapons. Let them come and test their strength against his own. The traitors would find out soon enough they had chosen the wrong side.

He watched as Hazel surged ahead of him, making directly for a pair of Enforcers who stood beside the locked gates to outside. That was good—so long as those doors stayed closed, no ships could leave to alert the Alfur. The pair barely saw her coming. Light bloomed in the darkness as they swung their batons, but Hazel moved like the wind itself, ducking and darting beneath their blows. She didn't use the Light itself to attack—she had only begun to discover her new powers—but rather wielded her old gladius.

Its edge proved no less deadly than a blade of Light.

Cries echoed through the corridor, quickly cut short. Hazel cut through the men like a hound in a hencoop, the growls she made more animalistic than human. Blood splattered her clothing as she spun, all but slicing the baton-wielding arm from the last man to face her.

Swallowing a sudden feeling of doom, Rydian spun to face a charging Enforcer—but Fatimah was faster still. Muscles rippling, the leopard leapt, its terrible jaws closing upon the man's throat. The Enforcer was dead before he knew what had struck him.

A sudden silence descended on the hanger. Seven Enforcers remained. They stood staring at Rydian and his companions, open fear on their faces. Hands trembled on glowing batons, the soft crackling of their energies the only sound in the broad room.

Then as one, the seven turned and ran. Not for the bay doors or the ruined gates through which Rydian and Hazel had entered but...

...but a panel on the far wall. Rydian had never noticed it before, but its function was immediately obvious. An alarm. Probably to alert the Alfur of trouble. If they reached it, all their plans would come to ruin before they had even begun.

Rydian drew on the Light and raised his fist. Energy was already gathering in this palm when he hesitated. He had been about to unleash that power against the panel, but what if that set off the alarm as well? Teeth clenched, he lowered his arm again and pulsed a message to Fatimah.

"Stop them," he said out loud at the same time.

Then he was charging across the platform. Artificial Light lit the space, leaving only the corners in shadow. It was a good three hundred feet wide and the Enforcers had a thirty second head start on their Light-imbued pursuers.

It wasn't enough.

The first fell with a cry as Fatimah slammed into his back, driving him face first into the stone floor. The big cat didn't pause to finish him. By far the fastest of the three of them, she bounded on, heading off the fastest of the pack. This one crumpled, screaming, as claws tore through his calf.

Then Rydian and Hazel were amongst the others. The last was just regaining his feet when Rydian's burning blade plunged through his spine. He died without a sound. And five remained.

Headed off by the big cat, the others were forced to turn and face the threat at their rear. Open terror was evident in their faces now. They might still have the numerical advantage, but these were men used to punching down. To dominating a population unable to resist, to fight back. Forced instead to suffer at the hands of their cruel overlords and their minions. To die, never knowing the taste of freedom.

For the first time in months, since that fateful day in the arena, Rydian allowed his rage to flow. The burning of his skin lit up the hanger as his blade found the neck of the first man to come against him—and carved through skin and flesh and bone. The Enforcer's body hit the floor a moment after his head.

Another fell, shrieking, as Hazel's gladius caught him in the chest. He thrashed on the ground, fingers clawing stone as he tried to crawl away, until a final blow to the neck silenced him.

Pain erupted in Rydian's side as one of the guards took advantage of his distraction to ram his energised baton into Rydian's stomach. A surge of energy went crackling through his veins. Grunting, he staggered a step, eyes wide, lips parted in the beginnings of a scream. Even the Enforcer looked surprised that his blow had landed.

But the man's luck proved short live. The Enforcer's

batons might have been enough to quill a threat from any normal human. But Rydian was no longer normal, and the amount of Light discharged by the weapon was little more than a spark compared to what burned within.

A grim smile touched his lips as he straightened. Before his foe could react, he had the man by the wrist. Twisting, he forced the baton up into the Enforcer's chin.

Light exploded from the baton, lighting his foe up like a solar flare. The man collapsed without a sound as Rydian released him. His smile grew as he faced the two that remained.

"Who's next?"

Suddenly on equal footing, the pair tried to back away, but a growl from Fatimah brought them up short. The last of the colour drained from their faces as they glanced back at the cat. Blood matted her yellow fur and her eyes burned. Behind her, the man she had taken down had been torn apart.

Thud. Thud.

The sound of the two batons striking the ground was shockingly loud in the open warehouse.

"Please!" The first of the men cried, raising his empty hands in supplication. "Please, don't hurt us sir."

"We were only trying to feed our families," the other added.

Rydian stared, mouth open. Blood was still pounding in his ears and that distant screaming had grown louder, niggling at the back of his mind. They screamed for him to kill, to strike down these men for what they were--traitors. But...no, no good could come from that rage.

Blinking, he realised his blade was still raised. He lowered it slowly, aware that he'd been only moments away from striking down two unarmed foes. Their words trickled into his consciousness. What had they said about feeding their families? He'd never considered the men behind the Enforcers—

The first man screamed as a flicker of Light came from Rydian's side. The cry cut off abruptly as Hazel sheathed her gladius in his throat. The other stumbled back, mouth open in horror, and Rydian raised a hand.

"Hazel, wait—"

He was too late. Blood splayed across the stone as she tore her blade loose from the first man and buried it up to the hilt in the chest of the second. He staggered back several steps as she released the hilt, eyes dark, watching as he crumpled to the floor.

Rydian stared, hand still outstretched to stop her. Slowly he lowered it and swallowed the lump in his throat. Light pulsed from beneath Hazel's skin, burning, consuming. He wondered then if he had made a terrible mistake, bringing his friends into this. If Hazel had already been lost...

"Hazel?" he said, his voice hesitant. "You good?"

She stood for a moment longer, looking down at the dying man. But as the last whispered gasps of his breath faded, she turned and looked at him. For a moment, he saw only darkness in her brown eyes. Then she blinked, and she returned, leaving him wondering if it had all been his imagination.

"We can't afford prisoners, Rydian," she rasped.

He swallowed. She was right, of course. Surrender meant prisoners. Prisoners had to be guarded. They couldn't afford to waste a single soul on that duty. Not with the odds already stacked against them. He looked again at the dead men. They had chosen this fate long ago, when they had sided with the Alfur against their own people. Whatever their reasons, that treason could not be so easily forgiven.

Grimacing, Rydian nodded his agreement. Together, they turned to seek out what they had come for...

...and breathed out a sigh when they saw the smaller ship nestled in the corner. All sleek edges and sharp corners, it glowed with a faint touch of Light from beneath. Exactly what Serena had told them to look for. Where the larger vessels that brought them from the gladiator complex were automated, a few of the smaller vessels could be flown by someone inside. Or at least, that was the theory. You needed an Alfurian Manus reader to pilot one.

A panel on the side opened the hatch on the side of the circular ship. What they found inside was like stepping into another world. Light glowed from a dozen panels, more complicated than anything Rydian had expected, and certainly stranger than the nearly empty vessels that ferried the gladiators between cities.

They moved to the front of the vessel, where the only chair was located. It looked out through transparent panels into the hanger. The pilot's seat, Rydian assumed from Serena's description. It was too large to be comfortable for a human, but Rydian would make do. More panels with glowing buttons and switches surrounded it, and for the first time he felt doubt. Serena had made piloting the ship seem simple enough, but she had been doing it for all her unnaturally long life.

As opposed to Rydian, who felt about as comfortable around Alfurian technology as a frog in a crockpot.

Too late to turn around now, Light Giver, Fatimah's rumbling wasn't exactly reassuring. But the beast was right.

Gathering his Light, Rydian raised his artificial hand. It had formed a Manus reader there, but its shape was like his old device. Now he concentrated on it, he watched it reform, growing larger, longer, and—he hoped—taking on the complicated inner workings of the Alfurian versions.

When the reworking had stopped, Rydian drew in a breath. There was a panel in the arm of the chair. Once he placed the Manus reader against that, there truly would be no going back.

Exhaling, he slumped into the soft cushions, and pressed his palm to the panel.

And the ship began to hum.

EIGHTEEN

The days ticked passed with an agonising lack of speed for Serena after she'd made contact with the humans. Minute by minute, hour by hour, she expected to hear the sounds of destruction from down the hallway, for the screams of the dying to reach her in her lonely cell. She'd made them promise not to harm her brethren...but they were humans. How much could one lonely Alfur trust their word?

She still wasn't even sure she'd made the right choice. She had mislead them. Not an outright lie, but...not the truth either. If she'd told them the truth, that the 'weapon' they were seeking was nothing more than fanciful equipment to pierce the Haze surrounding the planet...well, who knew what they would have done. She had a feeling that even without her help, they wouldn't have gone back to easy compliance.

But she hoped this way at least, they might both get

what they wanted. That she could contact her people off planet, and asked them to intervene on behalf the humans. To prevent a genocide they would surely oppose.

If not, well, then maybe Rydian and his crew could hold her father's precious equipment to ransom. He clearly valued it. Perhaps that would be enough.

But first the damned creatures had to *arrive*.

In the end, she heard nothing to betray the humans' arrival. The first clue she had that they'd reached the tower was her door beginning to glow a violent orange.

From there, she only had a few seconds to question the wisdom of inviting Light-imbued humans into her family home, before the doors exploded inward.

Reacting with the inhuman speed characteristic of her species, Serena stepped aside as the chunks of metal tumbled past. They slammed into her freshly recon-structed bed, leaving the frame and mattress in pieces for the second time in as many weeks.

Curses came from beyond the door, before two humans—and a *leopard*—stepped into her chambers. The first was immediately familiar. Rydian's hair had grown longer and his face had a haggard look about it, but his eyes still burned with the familiar determination that had drawn her attention, even before they had crossed blades in the arena.

"Princess," he greeted her calmly, as though the monster at his side was perfectly normal. "It is good to see you again."

The leopard lingered close to his side, as out of place

here as...well, two humans. Blood splattered its shining fur and Serena was surprised to sense the Light burning at its core. She hadn't realised the creatures carried such a potent force of their own. Perhaps if they had been more numerous...

Serena shook herself. This was not the time to allow her thoughts to wander. Two—scratch that, *three*—very dangerous creatures had just stepped inside her home. She needed to be on high alert.

Especially with the way the third human was staring at her.

This one was a female of the species. Her skin had been tanned by the relentless Goman sun and blonde hair hung down around her shoulders. Most frightening though was the Light that burned behind her brown eyes. Apparently, Rydian wasn't the only human who had freed their inner powers. That had...implications for the rest of her people, and it was all Serena could do to keep the fear from her face.

"So, you're Rotin," the woman said. The words came out more as a snarl than a coherent string of syllables.

"I was," Serena said.

Then ignoring the pair, she stepped past them, out into the corridor. Her guards lay on the ground to either side of the door. They didn't appear to have seen their assailants coming. Both were still breathing, thankfully. Lifting them each in one hand, she dragged them into the room. Only there did she pause. She'd hoped her escape would go unnoticed. But the ruined door put paid to that.

"You could have knocked, you know," she said archly.

The humans and their...pet had been surveying the wreckage themselves, but now they returned their attention to their Alfurian host. Considering the destruction they'd shown themselves capable of, Serena was surprised they had made it this far without raising a tower wide alarm. But then, it wasn't like the docking bays or corridors of her family tower were guarded. Afterall, it was impossible for a human to reach them up here.

Unless they had help.

"I thought you were locked in here," the human woman all but snapped.

"This is Hazel," Rydian said as the pair exchanged glares. "You might know her as Hawk."

Serena recognised the name, but did not say as much. "It only opens from the outside," she replied to the woman's statement.

"Oh." Rydian raised his eyebrows and glanced at the ruin they'd made of her door and bed. "Well...ah, sorry, I guess."

"It's only a door," Hazel replied shortly. "Doors can be replaced." Unfolding her arms, she stepped up close to Rotin. "People can't."

Despite herself, Serena swallowed, her hearts beating hard against her chest. This human was no friend of hers.

"Not so fearsome without your armour and helmet, are you?" the woman went on. A flicker of Light burned in the depths of her eyes. Suddenly Serena was wishing she'd insisted Rydian come alone.

Thankfully, Serena's training as the Goman heir came in useful for once. Her face remained a mask as she stared down the woman's hatred.

"I am what I am."

"What you are is a murderer."

"Today, I'm you're only friend in enemy territory," Serena replied. "Are you sure this is an argument you'd like to have just now?"

The woman narrowed her eyes. "Maybe I do," she hissed. "Maybe I'd like to know why so many had to die? Your hands are stained in our blood, Alfur. Why should we work with you now?"

Serena faced the woman down. This creature did not understand the ways of her people. She did not know what it took to gain the notice of an Alfurian prince, to make her father take note of the suffering of those so far beneath him.

"You do not understand..." Serena began, but the words died on her lips as she looked into those burning eyes.

"Don't I?" the gladiator snarled.

"My father...he never would have notice...without my..." she couldn't finish. Even to her own ears, the excuses sounded weak now, faint in the light of day.

Because she knew the truth. She hadn't fought in the arena for humanity.

She had done it because she enjoyed it.

The human seemed to know it too. She stared back at her, eyes dark, so dark Serena feared for a moment she looked into the eyes of some otherworldly creature, into the dark avengers from the human legends, those vengeful gods that lurked beneath the surface, waiting to strike down the surface creatures that dared disturb their slumber.

"You could have made your father pay notice to his people any time," the woman, Hazel, said softly, her voice dangerously low. "You could have made him see some other way. But like a spoilt teenager, you chose to rebel instead, to defy your dear old daddy." Her lips drew back in a sneer. "You know what, Rydian. I don't think we need her after all."

Serena flinched as the human suddenly raised her blade. Light blazed from her skin and she reached for a weapon she didn't have. Across the room, Rydian raised a hand, a cry on his lips, but even with all his power, he would be far too slow. Only Serena's own Light could save her now...

Laughter. Harsh and cold, it rang from Hazel's lips as she lowered the blade.

"So you do know fear," she cackled. "Good. Then know one day I will come for you, Rotin. And on that day, we will no longer be friends."

Silence fell. Lips pursed, Serena met the woman's eyes and saw the truth there. She nodded.

"Enough of this," Rydian hissed as the moment passed. "We can worry about grudges later. We have bigger concerns just now."

Serena nodded. Stepping around Hazel, she paused in the doorway to glance back at the pair. "Are you coming?"

"Obviously," Hazel snapped, arms crossed before her.

They followed her into the corridors. Pulling up her map of the tower, Serena led them towards the nearest stairwell. They had a long journey ahead of them, if her father was to be believed. The tower was huge, and the outpost would be near ground level.

"How did you disable her Manus reader?" she asked absently as they located the first set of stairs and started down.

"Falcon," Rydian grunted. "She knew a way to deactivate the devices. She just never told anyone, because of the whole Haze driving us insane side-effect."

"Until today," Hazel added, her voice cold. "Your friends on the surface are in for a fright."

Serena paused on the steps. "What?"

"That's how we got the ship without being noticed," Rydian explained grimly. "Johanas and the other gladiators are creating a...distraction."

"They unleashed their Light as well?"

Rydian nodded. Serena cursed beneath her breath.

"What?" he asked as she started down again, at a faster pace this time.

"We have to move quickly," Serena said breathlessly. "Your friends—and everyone in this city—are in danger."

"Huh?" Rydian's confusion was clear, but Serena didn't pause.

If her father was to believed, the humans were beginning to influence the Haze. If dozens of gladiators had suddenly been exposed to the Light...add to that the riots that had gripped Goma over the past months...

"My father believes the Haze is growing stronger," she explained as they moved. "Your friends are walking right into the teeth of the storm."

Hazel snorted. "We can handle ourselves—"

"No, you can't," Serena snapped. "You can barely keep yourself from running me through as it is—and I'm your only chance in this place. The Haze is going to burn through your friends like kindling. And then it will spread."

"Spread?" Rydian asked. "What do you mean?"

Serena exhaled. "The Haze is already beginning to affect the people of Goma, even with the Manus readers. After your stunt in the arena...there could be a mass failure."

The humans fell silent at Serena's words. She imagined the implications were just beginning to set in for them. An entire city of humans, suddenly possessed by Light—and a rage great enough to drive them all insane. There would be nothing left of Goma come morning.

"What do we do?" Rydian asked.

Serena was wondering that herself. Her father had mentioned the equipment was for studying the Haze, but he'd also said they'd been trying to manipulate it. Could it help them control the surge that even now must be spreading through the city? She had to hope so. Otherwise...

"We keep moving," she said softly. "And pray your friends can buy us some time."

"Enough time for what?"

"I'm still trying to work out that part."

NINETEEN

JOHANAS HAD ALWAYS LOATHED THE THOUGHT OF battle. Where others joyed in the bloodshed and mayhem of the arena spectacles, he had chosen to remain below with his father, to witness the aftermath of the injuries and death. Maybe that explained his aversion, at least in part. But it went deeper than that.

In truth, he couldn't see the logic in it. In the Goman barracks, he had heard other gladiators speak of the thrill of testing their strength and skill against another. To prove their power, their superiority over their fellow man.

Johanas had been in a few fights as a youth. Whether the other young men had seen him as a threat, or only wanted to 'test' themselves, the result had always been the same. The challenges had only stopped when he'd broken a man's jaw.

Perhaps that was why he'd never seen the attraction. Always before, he had found no challenge in the matchups. What did the giant Johanas have to prove when those who tried to fight him barely came up to his shoulders? When their thighs were only as thick as his arms?

Today though, Johanas had finally found himself a worthy challenger. Or rather, challengers.

He grinned as the Enforcers approached across the sands. His heart was racing, the Light pulsing in his veins, and finally, finally he could feel that sense of excitement. The rush that proceeded the kill. There were dozens of them, each armed with the crackling Light-batons that could stun or kill at a touch, depending on how much you had pissed off the wielder. Today, he had little doubt they would be set to kill.

It didn't matter. Not today. Not with the power Rydian Holt had shown him.

He shared a glance with the Mayenken woman at his side. The other gladiators remained below for now, but when the fighting broke out above, they would lead their individual factions against the Enforcers below the stadium. For now, that left Johanas and the Mayenken to deal with those above.

A wild grin stretched across the woman's lips as she raised a spear. Together they faced the oncoming threat, those men and women who had chosen the alien invaders over their own species.

And the killing began.

TWENTY

Unlike every other human on the planet, Rydian had actually been inside one of the Alfurian towers before this day. In fact, he'd been in this very tower. Yet he had still struggled to comprehend the wonders they had seen on their way to Serena's chambers. Every inch of the place was lit by the pale glow of Light, and long, clear windows of glass stretched along every corridor, looking out over the enormous expanse of the city.

His home looked small from so far above. And a fog hung about it, a gloom that only seemed all the darker for the luminescence of the sleek hallways of the Alfurian tower. Even the air tasted different. Refreshing, as though it had been cleansed of some corruption Rydian had never noticed before, but had been breathing all his life.

It was warmer too. Hot, even compared to the humid warmth of the jungle or city outside. He hadn't noticed that the last time. But then, he'd been in a half-stupor the last time he'd come here, deep in the thralls of the Haze. Barely sane, in truth. What a relief, his bond with Fatimah had been, to find himself clear headed once again.

Now though, he could feel the claws prodding against his skull, the tendrils of the Haze as they sought to reclaim him. Despite the great cat padding along at his side, it was returning. He prayed whatever treasure waited for them in the secret chambers of the Alfurian tower could save them. Otherwise...

They had both been sweating by the time they reached the end of Serena's directions and located her chamber. It had been a simple matter to disable the guards with his Light and blast open her door.

Now though, as they delved deeper and deeper into the tower, he found himself doubting. Serena hadn't been able to tell them exactly what it was that waited below. It could yet prove to be a trap, for all they knew. Some elaborate ploy to lure them away from their friends, to neutralise their threat without risking the city.

If that was the case, Rydian would bring this entire tower down on their heads before he fell.

Yet however much Hazel and his own logic screamed that Serena must surely plan to betray them, he trusted her. It made no sense. She was Rotin. The Alfur responsible for so many of his people's deaths. And heir to this entire section of the planet. Daughter to the creature that had ruled over Goma since the arrival of the Alfur however many hundreds of years ago.

Hazel was right. He should have killed her on the

sands when he'd had the chance. But he hadn't. And now she was trying to help them. It couldn't make much sense to her either, betraying her own kind on behalf of the humans they ruled. And yet here she was, leading them to a weapon that could see the Alfur overthrown.

"It is a very strange alliance this, isn't it?"

He jumped as the Alfur spoke and cast her a quick glance, wondering if perhaps her control over the Light gave her the ability to read minds. But no. Surely he would have stumbled upon that power by now, if that were true. He offered a frown instead. They were walking side by side, with Hazel and Fatimah bringing up the rear.

"What's so strange about an Alfurian princess allying herself with a pair of humans in order to overthrow her father's empire?"

Laughter rasped from the Alfur's throat. Rydian raised his eyebrows—he'd never seen one of her kind laugh before. The sound was not unlike a human's laughter, though it was higher in pitch, with a slightly metallic tang. Her skin brightened as she noticed him watching her.

"Perhaps it could become a new model for our peoples," she said after a moment. "That we might in the future work towards a united goal, rather than opposed."

A snort came from Hazel behind them. "Maybe one day the felines will make cause with the hounds."

The rumble from Fatimah's throat made it clear just what the great cat thought of *that* idea.

They continued. Deeper and deeper, until they left behind the great windows and well-lit corridors. In the depths of the Levaanton tower, darkness ruled. Only the walls remained to remind them they walked in Aflurian territory. All of pure steel, there were no signs of unwieldy joints and rivets. No human hand could have formed these towers. His people may have mined the materials from the ground, but they had been shaped by the Light, formed by masters. Even Rydian, had he developed a taste for architecture, could not have created such flawless panels. He was a blunt instrument with his power, while the Alfur for masters.

Nor could his mind have imagined the sprawling patterns that filled the corridors. The endless twirls and loops and spirals seemed more a part of the solid steel than anything carved or pounded into its surface. He had wondered at them since they'd left the ship in the empty docking bay, what they meant, but dared not ask their Alfurian guide.

Finally, they came to a place where even the patterns ended, and the walls turned from steel to stone. Here Serena hesitated, sharing a glance with Rydian and Hazel.

"The lowest part of the tower was built from stone, as foundations," she whispered, as though she feared being overhead. "These tunnels are recent."

As though summoned by the Alfur's words, there came a distant *crash*, as of a door being slammed. Far, far above, on another stairwell, another part of the tower. Probably nothing...

...but for the faint pattering of footsteps that followed.

Rydian swore beneath his breath and turned to the Alfur. "Who?"

She pursed her lips as her Manus reader began to pulse. "My father." She clenched her fist, cutting off the signal. "We had best be quick."

"At least we'll have a hostage when they catch us," Hazel muttered. Her hand rested on her sword hilt.

Grimacing, Rydian gestured for Serena to continue. He'd hoped they would reach the room before they were discovered.

This time though when they started off, the corridors were no longer silent. The far away thumping of feet on steel stairs chased after them. And as they continued down, down into the darkness, the sounds grew steadily louder.

But something else changed as well.

Something below them.

At first, Rydian couldn't figure out what it was, what had changed. But with each turn of the corridors, each fresh flight of stairs down through the stone, the sensation grew. A pulsing in his mind, a whisper against his consciousness, a breath across the back of his neck. And he knew what it was.

The Haze.

A rumble came from Fatimah as they realised. The sensation of something outside pressing against their minds was growing stronger as they neared whatever the Alfur had hidden in the bottom of their tower. He shivered as the pressure built. His bond with Fatimah resisted its whisperings—for now—and Hazel had only recently exposed herself to her own Light. Though...no, she hadn't become more violent, had she?

Recalling the Enforcers that had tried to surrender themselves, only to be cut down by her blade, Rydian couldn't be sure.

Only that *something* was below. Something that affected the Haze.

Maybe the same something that had driven his mother to turn her back on humanity. To betray the resistance. To kill Hazel's brother.

"I don't like this," Serena was saying, speaking so softly Rydian thought at first that she was talking to herself. "The guards will be on alert. They might react, even if it's just me they see. What if they destroy it?"

"You had better hope not," Hazel spoke from behind them. Steel rasped on leather as she drew her blade. "Or you're of no use to us, Alfur."

Serena paused a moment, glancing back at the gladiator. "Apologies. I do not know you well. Is this your normal level of aggression, or the Haze taking affect?" She glanced from Hazel to Rydian and raised her eyebrows.

Rydian looked at his friend. "You alright?"

Furrowing her brow, Hazel took long moments to reply—and when she did it was with a terse shake of her head. "Just a headache."

Nodding, he looked at Serena. The Alfur was still staring at Hazel, her lips twisted in what might have been an expression of concern. "We should reactivate her Manus reader."

"You'd like that, wouldn't you," Hazel snarled.

"Let's just keep going," Rydian interjected.

The others agreed, though only after a growl rumbled from the depths of Fatimah's throat as a reminder of her presence. Rydian smiled wearily at the big cat as the two women took the lead. They turned together towards the next set of stairs.

I...do not like the sense of this place.

Rydian was almost surprised to hear the cat speak again. It had remained largely silent since reaching the city, as though something about the place was pressing upon its mind. Rydian could feel it too, that heady presence of the Haze. He hoped it really was whatever lay beneath them, and not as Serena had feared, and Johanas's uprising was having...side effects for the rest of the city.

I know, he replied. He clenched his fist, feeling the power there. *Be on alert...*

He wasn't sure what they needed to be on alert for. The danger was behind them, wasn't it?

"Why are you doing this?" he asked suddenly.

The words hung in the air, and ahead, Serena paused. Her face was dim when she glance back, the Light beneath her translucent skin faded to be barely visible in the gloom. His hand was far brighter.

"Because what we have done to your people is wrong," she said before continuing on the path.

The corridors had grown narrow now, leaving them

only enough room to walk comfortably in single file. Rydian hurried after the alien creature.

"You really care, don't you?" he asked.

They entered yet another stairwell, this one entirely dark. The artificial Lights had grown ever rarer as they ventured into the depths. Now they appeared to have vanished entirely. Rydian coaxed extra Light to his artificial hand to light their path. A whisper of thanks carried back to him from Hazel, who had taken the lead.

"Should I not?" Serena sounded genuinely perplex.

Rydian shrugged. "No Alfur I have ever met cared a jot whether I lived or died."

She pursed her lips as she glanced back at him. "I... understand," she replied. "For too long, my people have thought ourselves your saviours. Protecting you from the Haze. My father and the other princes believed that gave us power over your lives. It was hubris. We should have been allies. United, we could have solved the problem of the Haze once and for all, for both our kinds."

Rydian took a moment to puzzle over her words. "What is the Haze to the Alfur?"

This time Serena came to a complete stop. "Damn," she murmured when Rydian and Hazel stopped along with her. "Sometimes I forget..."

"What aren't you saying, Alfur?" Hazel growled. Her blade was still unsheathed. It glittered in the Light of Rydian's blade as she raised it towards Serena.

To the creature's credit, she did not flinch. Though he supposed Serena had faced enough naked steel during her time in the arena. Even so, he sensed she was not altogether...comfortable faced with Hazel's weapon.

"It is nothing," she said, before her voice took on a wry note, "only...a minor issue for a space faring race such as ours." She made a gesture, as though to take in the air around them. "The Haze is more than just a problem for human minds. It interferes with our equipment when our ships try to leave the atmosphere."

Rydian blinked. "You're trapped here?"

Serena pursed her lips. "Some of us have never even seen our home world."

Rydian's heart pulsed. This information...changed everything. Always before, humanity had assumed that attacking the Alfur was futile. Even if they somehow gained control of the towers, even if they killed every one of the species on the planet, that only meant more would come, seeking vengeance. But if none could come or go...

He shook himself. They had other issues just now—such as how to cope with the growing pulse of the Haze. And the footsteps that sounded ever closer from the corridors above them.

"This place," he said instead, "it has something to do with the Haze, doesn't it?"

"I...think so, yes," Serena said hesitantly.

It would have to be enough. Their time was already growing short. He nodded for Serena to continue. She obeyed, striding forward around the next bend in the corridor...

...and coming to an abrupt stop.

In the narrow corridor, Rydian almost walked into her back. Cursing, he made to squeeze past her to see what had caused the delay, but she raised a translucent arm to bar his way. He was forced to crane a head around her shoulder instead to see what lay beyond the tall Alfur.

The hall was silent, empty. But at its end, Light seeped from beneath a sleek, metallic door.

"We're here," Serena whispered.

Rydian's heart pounded hard in his chest. He hadn't needed her to speak the words. He could *sense* it. The source of the disturbance he and Fatimah had sensed, the distortion in the Haze, it came from behind that door.

"But where are the guards?" the Alfur questioned.

"What does it matter?" Hazel snapped.

Before either Rydian or Serena could react, she had shouldered her way past them and was advancing down the corridor towards the door. Belatedly, they chased after her, the big cat padding along at the rear. Rydian hissed for Hazel to wait so they could assess their options, but the gladiator had cast aside all caution. As they approached the steel-panelled door, she raised her hand.

Rydian realised what she was doing a second before the spark appeared between her fingers. He opened his mouth to cry out a warning. The Haze was far too strong here for them to be using their Light so profusely. Better Serena use her Manus reader than Hazel experiment with her own power here in this place.

But it was already too late. Light burned as the spark

burst to life in Hazel's palm. Then with a crackling burst of power, it leapt from her to strike the door.

Steel shrieked and twisted, then gave way before the power, sending a chunk of metal tumbling into the room beyond. A heavy *crash* followed as it came to rest. Light spilled into the gloom of the corridor, though this came not from Hazel, but whatever lay within the hidden chamber. A shadow appeared within the Light.

Rydian sensed Serena grow tense, heard the whispered intake of Hazel's breath as she inhaled, caught the whiff of molten steel in his nostrils. None of it could tear his eyes from the silhouette that had appeared within the Light. From the person that stepped from the brilliance.

From the woman that stood suddenly, impossibly before him.

"Mom?"

TWENTY-ONE

Blood dripped from Johanas's blade.

Before today, he would have grieved its owner.

Now he gloried in it.

It was the Haze, he knew. He just no longer cared. Afterall, did he not have a right to anger? Had not his entire life been one of service? Of slavery to a supposedly superior race. Hadn't they made him into a killer? Turned him into the beast that now threatened their precious peace.

Today, the Alfur reaped the fruit they had sowed.

Though so far, only human blood had been spilled, he knew they would come soon. Half of their Enforcers were already dead. Their blood spilled the sand around Johanas, their bodies lying still at his feet. The Mayenken woman lay with them. He had never gotten her name. She had been just like all the others, in the end. Unable to compete, to match his power.

Now he stood alone against the dozen Enforcers who remained.

They trembled as Johanas approached.

And the crowd roared.

How quickly the pathetic creatures had forgotten their hatred. He could not blame them for it, for loathing the cowardly creature he had been. But he could loath them in return for their own weakness. For cowering all these years beneath the yolk of the Alfur. For standing by even now as he fought for their freedom.

Truth was, the Alfur was right about one thing. These pathetic creatures did not deserve their freedom.

But that was a concern for another day.

Today, Johanas had Enforcers to kill.

The Light pulsed inside him as another of the enemy came for him. He avoided a vicious swing of the man's baton—he'd already felt their bite this day, and while he'd survived, it wasn't an experience he wished to repeat. The air crackled as the charged weapon passed within an inch of his face. Then it was Johanas's turn to attack.

Empowered by the Light, his great sword *hissed* as it cut the air.

And the Enforcer hit the sands in two pieces.

Another tried to throw down her weapon and surrender. The old Johanas would have paused at the woman's actions. Would have granted leniency, shown compassion. That Johanas had been weak. Had allowed to Alfur to rule his life. To control him.

The woman died screaming for her treachery.

And Bloodlust continued his bloody campaign against the minions of the Alfur.

Only when the last of the Enforcers fell did he finally give himself leave to pause. Slamming his blade deep into the sands, he stood back and looked around at his adoring crowd. His breath came in gasps. His heavy frame had been left to rot these past months. Not even the Light within was enough to sustain him forever.

The humans in the stands were all on their feet at his victory. Now though, their cheers slowly began to fade. They looked to one another. Bloodlust could sense their doubt. What came next, now that the gladiators had rebelled? Nervous eyes turned to the skies. The traitor would be punished surely, but what of the crowd that had cheered him on?

As though they had been waiting for that very moment, a silver ship rose above the stands of the arena. Screams rang through the crowd as men and women threw themselves to the ground. Bloodlust ignored them. His eyes were set on this new challenger. He rested a hand upon the pommel of his sword, and smiled.

Rage burned within him.

Rage at the beings that hovered in the sky above them.

Chaos spread around the stands as the humans tried to flee. But the Alfur's minions had sealed the gates long ago. Sealed their own fates, locking themselves in with Bloodlust. But they had not known what they faced then.

The Alfur knew.

And cowards that they were, they would not fight him on his terms.

A great crystal orb had been mounted at the front of the Alfurian vessel. Bloodlust bared his teeth as Light began to gather there.

Cowards, he thought.

And began to gather Light of his own.

So far he had used it only to enhance his own movements. To be faster, stronger, more aware than the men and women who came against him. Now he would use it as the Alfur did, as a blast of energy that would destroy anything that stood before him.

The power gathered within, burning, searing at his veins, until he felt it must burst from him. Above, the ship's device grew brighter. Legends told of weapons possessed of the Alfur that could level cities. Bloodlust did not care. Today, he would meet the Alfur's fire, and emerge victorious—

Boom!

An explosion rocked the stadium. For a moment, Bloodlust could not understand what had happened. A second *crash* echoed from the stands as the Aflurian ship fell from the sky and slammed into the ground, showering the gladiators gathered there with sand.

Bloodlust stood and stared at the fallen vessel. An enormous wound had been open in its side, as though some giant knife had carved through the strange metal. The scorch marks around the edges revealed the true source. Light. Someone had struck the ship down before either he or the Alfur could unleash their own powers.

"You really thought you could match it, didn't you?"

He turned as the light footsteps of a woman approached. Falcon's face was grey, her lips pursed in a grim scowl as she walked up to Bloodlust. He was surprised to see her. The plan had been for her to remain below, rather than risk losing her to the Haze. Apparently, the plan had changed.

"Arrogance presides the fall," she added. Her sapphire eyes looked past him, to the broken ship.

Bloodlust scowled. "I had things in hand, Falcon."

A grim laughter came from the woman's throat. "That blast would have levelled this entire stadium," she said. Movement came from the broken wreckage of the ship. The Goman champion drew her sword. Light blazed to life beneath her skin and finally she looked at him. "I hope you're ready, Johanas."

"It's Bloodlust."

"No, it isn't," Falcon grimaced, "but we can talk about that later. If we survive. Just now, it looks like we've royally pissed off our overlords."

Bloodlust turned and saw that it was true. They emerged one by one from the wreckage, skin ablaze with Light, fine sabres similar to the one Rotin had wielded at the ready. One, two, half a dozen. Even with their Light, that was too many.

A smile spread across his lips. Just the challenge he needed to truly test his ability.

Reaching out, he plucked his greatsword from the sands. Raising it above his head, he roared a challenge to his Alfurian foes.

And charged.

TWENTY-TWO

"Mom?"

The word was like a thundercrack. Hazel stood frozen in the corridor, staring at the woman that had emerged from the hidden room. If not for Rydian's exclamation, she might not have recognised the woman responsible for destroying her life.

Jasmine Holt had aged. Before, the freedom fighting leader of the resistance had carried an exuberance about her, an enthusiasm for life, for the future. There was no sign of that energy in the woman standing before Hazel now. Her blonde hair seemed closer to white now, the life faded from its long strands. Wrinkles creased the skin around her eyes...eyes which stared at them without light or love or life.

"Oh son," even Jasmine Holt's voice was different from how Hazel remembered it. "You should not have come here."

The words sounded dull, depressed. There was no excitement for her long-lost son, for an unexpected reunion.

Yet none of that mattered to Hazel.

"I saw you die," she rasped. She had. She was sure. Chaos had erupted when the Alfur had broken into the facility, when they had unleashed their Manus readers. She had seen her brother fall, seen a body crumple...*had* it been Jasmine?

"I thought you were dead?" Rydian whispered.

His voice was hoarse, his eyes wide, unblinking. The reason for his shock was obvious. For him, this was an impossible moment, a fragile spark in a dark room.

But all Hazel could see was red.

"You're supposed to be dead!"

This time, everyone heard her. Her scream rang from the stone ceilings, her rage and hatred and betrayal, all given voice. She was shaking—trembling at the injustice of it all. All this time, her only consolation, the only thing that had let her sleep at night after her brother's death, was that his murderer lay in the ground with him. It had been a cold, insufficient form of justice, but justice all the same.

Now, seeing her standing there before them, that sad frown upon her lips.

"There is no justice in this world," she spoke the words in a whisper.

This time Hazel didn't need her sword. The anger blazing within would be the weapon of her vengeance. It surged, burning, searing, screaming to be unleashed. Power to control. Power to destroy.

She raised her hand. That was all the permission the Light needed. Suddenly the fire was no longer inside her. Blinding brilliance lit the hallway as it gathered in her palm.

And as the fire crackled, Jasmine met Hazel's eyes. Understanding reflected back from their icy depths. The woman made no move to flee, to escape Hazel's wrath. Lips pursed in a frown, she watched the Light gather.

With a scream, Hazel unleashed her power, sending it against the woman that had killed her brother, that had destroyed her life.

Boom!

She stumbled as her Light exploded. The earth trembled and for a heartbeat the very air seemed to be aflame. A ringing began in her ears as the glow faded, as the corridor returned to the shadows. Hazel blinked, struggling to see through the stars dancing before her eyes.

Jasmine remained in the centre of the corridor, unmoved.

But now Rydian stood between them, hands raised, Light blazing in his eyes. He panted gently, as though what he'd done had cost something. A rumble came from his side as the great leopard crouched, its eyes fixed on Hazel. It looked...hungry.

"Hazel, please, don't."

She blinked. Blood thundered in her skull. Light

blazed in her fingertips, seared through her veins, screamed into her mind...

...she gasped, blinking, struggling to breath through the pain, through the rage. She was still in the corridor, still surrounded by the cold stone. So why did it feel so hot?

Looking up, she saw again Rydian standing before her. Why did he have that frown on his face? And...why was he protecting the murderer behind him...

"*You*," she hissed. "I knew you would betray us." She clenched her fist, and Light streamed between her fingers.

"I would never betray my people," he replied. "You know that, Hazel. You know me. Please, this is the Haze. All of it. Let my mother speak. Let her explain." He sounded hesitant with those last words, as though he did not entirely believe them himself. Glancing back, he looked at where his mother still stood in silence. "Right, mom...?"

He trailed off as another sound reach them. Footsteps.

"It doesn't matter, son." Jasmine's voice was toneless, without any hint of emotion. Her eyes remained on Hazel instead of her son. "She can strike me down if she chooses. I deserve it, and so much more for my crimes. For all our crimes."

Despair. That was the emotion in the woman's eyes, Hazel realised. It gave her pause. What was going on here? She glanced over her shoulder, checking for signs of their pursuers. The footsteps were close now, and shadows danced in the gloom beyond their corridor. They had only minutes before the other Alfur reached them.

"Mom, what are you talking about?" Rydian drew her attention back to the traitor. "I know the Haze made you do terrible things—"

"The Haze made me do nothing," Jasmine interrupted, her voice suddenly harsh. She held up her hand, revealing the Manus reader there. It glowed, though instead of the usual soft white, its Light was tainted green. "The Haze is not responsible for our vile deeds. It only reveals our ugly truth, the evil we carry in our hearts."

She took as step towards them then, her eyes harsh, lips drawn back in a sneer. "Do it, girl. I know you want to. Destroy me, like I destroyed your brother." She laughed, the sound as cold as those sapphire eyes. "He begged me to save you, you know. As I knelt beside his body, watching the blood bubble from his lips, he pleaded for my help."

Hazel couldn't look away from Jasmine, couldn't close her ears to those awful words. They might have been lies, taunts to force her to act, to be reckless. It didn't matter.

Something broke. Something went *snap* inside her. Some small, fragile part of Hazel that had still believed in humanity.

Screaming, Hazel unleashed her Light.

Sizzling, crackling, her power rent the air and rushed towards Jasmine. But again, Rydian stood between Hazel and the target of her fury. Teeth bared, he raised his hand towards the oncoming energy...

...and the corridor went dark.

Hazel blinked. What...had happened? She stood

staring at where her Light had been just moments before, but it had vanished as though it had never been. Vanished into Rydian's outstretched hand, as though he had absorbed all that power, all the strength of her fury.

A sudden wave of nausea swept through Hazel. Her knees trembled. She had put all her strength, all her energy, all her Light into that attack. And Rydian had absorbed it as though it was of no consequence. Stars burst across her eyes, and suddenly she was on her knees, swaying, staring up at her friend.

How could he have betrayed her...again.

His cheek twitched as he stared back at her, the only sign of stress on his sun-kissed face.

"Well, doesn't seem wise."

Hazel frowned. Who was that...

"Father!"

That was the Alfur they had kidnapped, wasn't it? Hazel swayed on her knees. Fearing she would fall, she stretched out her hands so they pressed against the ground. The stone was cool beneath her palms. Stone. Had they travelled so far down the tower that they were beneath the ground? That would be...good. Good to finally rest with her Gods.

"Daughter, I must say, I am disappointed."

"I can explain..."

A ringing was sounding in Hazel's ears, a screeching, wailing pressing against her mind. White spots filled her vision so that she could not make out the speakers. Both spoke with the strange, almost musical accents of the Alfur.

"But not surprised," that other voice continued.

Hazel swayed on her hands and knees, still trying to make out the speaker. Its owner carried the weight of authority about it, but her sluggish mind refused to work.

"What are we all doing here, Levaanton?"

That was Rydian. He was doing his best to appear unflustered, but Hazel knew him. She could hear the strain in his voice. Maybe absorbing her attack had cost him more than she'd thought.

"A very good question, Rydian Holt."

Levaanton. The Alfurian prince of Goma. Hazel's heart clenched and she reached for her Light...but found only agony. Fiery Light burned inside her, but it was no longer under her control. It twisted and turned, searing wherever it touched, until all she could do was open her mouth to scream...

She only managed a moan as she slumped against the ground. Cold stone pressed against her cheek, but it did little to quench the flame within. The rage. The hatred.

An audible sigh came from somewhere above.

"Ms Holt, would you be so kind?"

Footsteps approached. Hazel tried for a growl, tried to push the soft hands that reached for her away, but whatever had happened to Jasmine Holt, it had not stolen her strength. Soft hands became like iron shackles as she gripped Hazel hard by the wrist. A second later, a terrible pain stabbed through her palm, as though a dagger had been driven through her hand.

A scream tore from Hazel and she reached for her dwindling Light. Little enough, but surely it could help repel the woman's assault...

...but suddenly, even that remnant glow was denied to Hazel.

"Good, good, it would have been a shame to waste all that potential."

Blinking, Hazel found her vision suddenly clear. The screaming in her mind had vanished, the agony too, gone as surely as though it had never been. There was a warmth in her hand where she'd felt the stabbing pain. Her heart clenched as she looked down and saw the glint of steel and crystal. A second Manus reader. This one still glowed with an inner Light.

Her anger returned in an instant, but when she looked up, Jasmine Holt had already retreated. Their eyes met, and Hazel thought she glimpsed regret there. She must have been imagining things.

"Very good," the calm voice of an Alfur came from behind Hazel. "Now, where were we?"

Turning, she set eyes on the prince of Goma. He was taller than his daughter, his skin bright with Light. Golden eyes glinted in the gloom. A dozen Alfur stood at his back, Manus readers held at the ready. No wonder Rydian hadn't attacked yet.

"You were going to tell us why we're all here, Father,"

Serena replied. Her voice was taut, but despite her anger, she did not meet her father's eyes.

So much for on our side, Hazel couldn't help but think.

"Ah yes," Aiden Levaanton smiled. On his pale, inhuman face the emotion held no joy. He held out a hand towards the illuminated doorway. "After you, Daughter."

TWENTY-THREE

"A_FTER YOU, D_AUGHTER."

The words rang in Serena's ears. They were a trap, surely. A jest. But that smile on her father's face, there was no joy there. No humour. What was going on here?

"What's in there?" she whispered, her eyes never leaving the matching gold of her father's.

He laughed. "I tried to protect you from this, Daughter, but you would not be deterred. Come now, do not tell me you are having second thoughts now?"

Serena shivered. Looking into her father's eyes, she saw no flicker, no hint of the truth. It was terrifying. Somehow, her father had lied to her. She'd thought herself too intelligent, thinking she could manipulate him, but he had known all along. Known exactly what to say to her, what to promise, to lure her here.

Her eyes drifted to the room at the end of the corridor. The one from which the human woman had emerged.

Jasmine Holt. She was meant to be dead. Another lie. How? Her father claimed she had adopted too many human characteristics, but this was beyond anything she had done. He had lied to their entire race.

So what, then, was beyond that door?

"You have brought us all here, Daughter," Aiden continued to speak. His voice was a whisper, carrying with it the depths of his regrets. Another lie? "You led these humans to this place. It is too late for you to turn back now."

Serena swallowed. "If I have done wrong...let the punishment fall on my shoulders. The humans—"

"The humans...have made their own...choices," Rydian interrupted her. His voice was a growl, though he panted between words. At his side, the great leopard stood unnaturally still, though its golden eyes were fixed to her father.

She met his eyes and saw the fire there, the Light that glowed within, and swallowed. Her father might think this situation under control, but he underestimated Rydian at his own risk. She looked back to her father.

"I only did what I thought was right, Father. What you taught me to do. To protect the lives of those placed under our care."

"Ah daughter, you understand nothing of the precipice upon which we stand," he replied. Clasping his arms behind his back, he advanced towards them. The Alfur at his back advanced with him. "But then, I have only myself to blame."

Serena's hearts throbbed in her ears. "And why is that, Father?" she growled. "By the stars, tell me what secrets could justify genocide?

His expression did not change. "The truth of how we all came to be here."

"You already told us," Rydian snapped, injecting himself between Serena and her father.

Serena welcomed the interruption, for at last her father's face showed some emotion. Though it was not fear or sadness or even remorse, but open disgust.

"And if only that had been enough for you," he snarled. "Talamh might have peace."

"You lied, didn't you?" Rydian pressed.

"Son..." the woman, Jasmine, tried to intervene. "Son, please..."

Rydian retreated a step from her. Eyes wide, he looked from his mother to Serena's father. "Why are you defending him? What on Talamh is going on here? Why would you stand with this creature, after all the crimes he has committed against us?"

"Because there are other crimes that must be answered for," the woman said sadly.

Serena's hearts were racing now. "What is this all about, Father?"

"That's just it, isn't it?" Aiden Levaanton said. "It is all about them. It has always been about them." He shook his head. "I will play no more games. Had it been me, I would have sent our ships to destroy you and your rebel friends. Instead, at the bidding of the hero Jasmine, I offer you a choice: submit to our Manus readers, return to your city and ask no more questions and leave the Alfur to rule Talamh in peace."

"I'm not hearing much of a choice," the woman, Hazel, had regained her feet now. Her fists were clenched, but Light no longer seeped between her fingers. The Manus reader Jasmine had administered was apparently doing its job.

Not so for Rydian though. Raw Light spilt from his eyes, seeped from his skin. He was trembling now, his entire body shaking.

"What's the second option?" he ground out.

"Take the first, son," Jasmine interrupted.

Serena shivered as she saw something in the woman's eyes. They seemed drained, absent of life. What had been done to this woman all these months since her disappearance?

"The second choice I offer is the truth. Raw, unrevised knowledge that can never be taken back. As your mother can attest."

"Why would we be afraid of the truth..." Hazel started. She trailed off when Serena's golden eyes turned towards her.

Serena was gripped by a sudden terror as she watched her father. What had he said...the truth...about how they had come to be there? But...surely not...surely the elders could not have kept such a secret? They were a truthful race, honest. Not like the lying humans...

She swallowed. That was it, wasn't it? Everything

their society had been built on was a lie. Their nobility of spirit. The grace with which they had saved humanity, instead of enslaved. How the Alfur had protected the sorry creatures, even as they ground their species further and further into the mud. The Alfur had lied to themselves in a thousand little ways over the decades and centuries.

So why not this as well?

Her father was looking in Serena's direction again. She met his eyes, defiant. She knew the decision was not hers to make, but she wanted him to know she would have chosen the truth anyway. Whatever it was, it could not be worse than ignorance. Then standing by in silence as her kind committed genocide.

"This is your final chance, humans," her father continued, ignoring the fleeting questions of the humans. "I suggest you take the first. Return to your city. We will not come for you. We will not persecute you. So long as you behave."

The humans stood frozen, looking at one another in sudden doubt.

"Please, son," Jasmine whispered. She stood behind Aiden, barring the way to the room beyond. "Please, turn back. I wish I could, but it is already too late for me."

Rydian frowned, his brow furrowing in concern, but this time there was no give in the human man. "I am sorry, mom, but I cannot. Too many people have sacrificed for us to turn back now."

He looked to Serena's father. "Show us."

Serena's father inclined his head. "Very well." With the words, he turned and swept past Jasmine Holt, into the room beyond.

The others hesitated only a moment before following him—Rydian first, then Hazel. Jasmine lowered her eyes and scrunched them closed, as though it hurt just to witness what would come next. But as the pair moved past, they opened again, lifting to seek out Serena. They met, blue eyes of humanity to golden Alfur.

"I'm sorry," the woman whispered.

And the screaming began.

TWENTY-FOUR

Fighting the Alfur was not like...fighting humans.

Bloodlust realised that in the first clash of steel weapons. These were not creatures of flesh and blood alone, frail and breakable. Light fortified their lithe bodies, gifting them strength beyond their frail limbs. Where against the Enforcers, none could stand against the powerful blows of Bloodlust's sword, this time sparks flashed as an Alfur's blade met his own. And this time it was Bloodlust who found himself staggering backwards from the impact.

His hands turned numb, but thankfully he managed to hold onto the leather-wrapped hilt. Unable to contain his shock, he looked from the weapon to the Alfur.

The creature's cold silver eyes stared back at him. A smile stretched its lips.

It attacked.

If before he had been surprised by its strength, now Bloodlust was shocked by the creature's ferocity. It practically exploded from the sand, its razor-sharp blade flashing for his throat. Not even the Light was enough to save him from that speed. Thankfully, he had another trick up his sleeve. Drills long hammered into him by Aureli's training kicked in. Instinctively, his greatsword flashed up to deflect the blow—then lashed out in a riposte that almost took the Alfur's head from its shoulders.

Only its own supernatural speed saved the creature from that fate, as it twisted backwards, leaving Bloodlust's blade to cleave only empty air.

He growled as the creature began to laugh. The smile on its lips grew, its eyes dancing as it began to circle—

Suddenly the creature stiffened as a gladius took it through the back. Blue blood burst from the wound as the blade was withdrawn, but before the creature could stagger back to its friends, the gladius struck again. Its head made a solid *thump* as it struck the sands.

Resting her blade on her shoulder, Falcon strode forward to join Bloodlust again. "No sense playing fair with this lot," she said. "Kill them however you can."

"I had it in hand," Bloodlust growled.

"Whatever." Falcon spat on the body at her feet. "It's dead. Stop playing by their rules. Now we only have five left to kill."

He grunted his agreement, eyes turning to the remaining creatures. Their flesh had brightened with the death of their brother. Anger burned in their eyes. Apparently, the creatures weren't impressed with their sportsmanship. They spread out in a semicircle around the pair of gladiators and raised their Manus readers.

Bloodlust braced, gathering the Light he had prepared earlier for the ship. He might not have the power to compete with one of those vessels, but surely these sorry creatures he could match. Afterall, they had to consume their Light. He could make his own.

Power swept through him. The power these creatures had for so long denied him. That he had denied himself. That knowledge fed his rage, fuelled his need to destroy, to cast down these retched creatures that dared to call themselves overlords.

Flames lit his palm, burning pure white. The Manus readers of the enemy glowed as well, building in power, but they could not match the fire of Bloodlust's fury. Could not match his rage. His hatred.

"Feels good, doesn't it?" That was Falcon.

Bloodlust blinked, momentarily distracted. He struggled to hold onto the fire he had built. Falcon stood at his side, sword still resting on one shoulder, the blue blood of the dead Alfur dripping slowly onto her shirt. Lips pursed, face pale, her eyes were fixed on the enemy—but she had made no effort to gather any Light of her own.

"Oh, don't mind me." She must have sensed his hesitation, for her gaze did not flicker. "I do that one more time, I'll be insane for sure." Her face twitched, her lips drawing back to reveal clenched teeth. "But you go ahead. I'm sure you'll be fine. Gods below I could use a drink."

The words hung in the air a moment before Bloodlust could process them. Pity touched him, that she refused to embrace her power. There was no Haze, he had realised, only humanity's rightful rage at their long imprisonment. If that was insanity, so be it.

He turned back to the Alfur. Thankfully, they seemed entranced by Falcon's casual manner, as though they couldn't quite understand the strange woman. He didn't blame them. Bloodlust didn't either.

But he did have a burning ball of Light gathered between his fingers.

It was time to see what he could do.

TWENTY-FIVE

Serena flinched as the screaming began. The sound echoed loudly in the corridor, a grating, haunting cry that didn't seem entirely...natural.

It was a moment before she realised that was because the voices *weren't* real. Or at least, they had not been projected from any human or Alfurian throat. They were projections, sounds cast by the Light or devices powered by the Light.

A frown touched her forehead. She was the last to step into the chamber, to see whatever lay within. Her human companions hadn't made a sound after disappearing into the brilliance of that room. All that remained was the awful, awful screaming.

Serena swallowed. She could still turn around. Still flee this hidden darkness in the pit of her family tower. Pretend she had never stood on this precipice.

But no, she had come too far. Men and Alfur were dying around them. Dying because of events she had set in motion.

She couldn't turn around now.

Squaring her shoulders, Serena Levaanton stepped into the Light.

The machines were the first thing she noticed. They filled the room, whirring softly with the Light thrumming within, though the sound was all but drowned out by the projected screams. If not for her Alfurian senses, she would not have even noticed it. These must be the machines her father had said they had moved, the ones he'd claimed were used to monitor the Haze—and try to pierce through the veil to contact the outside world.

That, of course, had been a lie.

Only now Serena knew why.

The Light screens were the second thing she noticed. They filled the room. It had been their brilliance that had spilled out into the shadows of the corridor.

The videos and images playing across those screens answered every question she had ever asked of her father.

They showed the world beyond Talamh. The galaxies beyond the dark trappings of the Haze. The universe that had been denied to her people for a thousand years.

Her father's lie hadn't been in what this room did.

The lie had been in why it was hidden.

In why the council had kept it from her people.

And why they had been so terrified the humans might get their hands on it.

"What is this..." Rydian whispered.

"This room is our sole source of communication with the outside universe," her father said quietly. His golden eyes watched the images, listened to the screams coming from any number of the screens. "We monitor the channels for messages. For distress signals and calls for help. For any word from others of our kind."

He turned from the screens then, and his eyes met Serena's.

"In the hundreds of years we have watched and listened, no one has ever escaped to call for our help."

Turning, he looked at Jasmine Holt. She swallowed, then raising her Manus reader, she made a gesture towards the screens. Several grew larger. Those with video and the clearest images. And sounds.

Serena shuddered. Now she saw the truth, those screams cut to the depths of her soul.

On the remaining screens, she witnessed her people suffering. Thousands upon thousands of them. Bound in chains, bowed low by starvation, their flesh torn and broken by whips, the Alfur were a broken people. Their skin dulled by exhaustion, they worked in the depths of broken darkness, stumbled across plateaus with great blocks of stone upon their backs, died by the hundreds as they fought and died to beasts such as the one that stalked at Rydian's side. Upon every screen, every galaxy, every world, the Alfur suffered.

And on every world, one species stood over them, whip in hand.

Humanity.

"Now you see, son," Jasmine Holt's voice was a broken thing. Her pale face reflected the images upon the screens.

They all saw.

On each screen, the humans burned bright with Light. It shone across a thousand worlds, a hundred galaxies, across an entire universe. Unquenchable. Power to enslave. Power to control. Power to rule. They wielded it without mercy.

Even as they watched, an Alfur on the screen fell, her strength at an end. Her eyes were a dull copper, her skin faded to grey. Serena's hearts ached as she watched her sisters suffering, watched as she raised a pleading hand to the human that stood over her...

Light descended on the Alfur. Shaped into a terrible whip, it did not kill, but the razor edge cut deep into the Alfur's back. Blue blood splayed across the ground as another scream rang through the room. Gasping, sobbing, the Alfur crawled towards the item she had dropped—some kind of steel box—and struggled to lift it.

Serena shook with rage. With sorrow. With...hatred. Hatred for the being that stood over her sister. For a creature that could be so desperately, horribly cruel. For a species that could have enslaved her entire race...

"I don't believe it," Rydian whispered. The human stood nearby, his eyes wide, shining with the Light. "It's... it's just more lies..."

"No, son," Jasmine whispered. "This is the truth. This is why I could not let the others find this place. Why I had to turn against the other leaders." She swallowed. "They would have...reached out to those monsters. They would have brought them here..."

Serena shuddered. She finally understood. This was why her father and the elders had lied. Why they'd kept the truth from everyone—even their heirs. They hadn't come here as explorers. They had come here as refugees, fleeing a terrible, barbaric race.

"How?" Serena rasped. "How could you keep this from us?" Her hearts were racing, her blood burning, the Light within shifting, sizzling.

"Peace," her father whispered. "So that our children could grow up without fear. That we might begin again on this planet."

"What...then...I don't understand," Rydian was still shaking his head. His skin was bright with the Light within and his eyes were glazed, distant. "How...

"Humanity has ruled the universe since their ascension," Aiden Levaanton said softly. "Thousands of years have passed beneath their rule, and each generation their cruelty only grows. All who resist are destroyed."

"I...no...it's not possible..." Rydian whispered. "All of this, all because of the Haze?"

To everyone's surprise, Aiden Levaanton threw back his head and laughed. The humans jumped as the harsh sound echoed alongside the screams. Even Serena flinched. There was ice in her father's eyes as he stared down at the human.

"The Haze?" he whispered. "There is no Haze out

there, Rydian Holt." He made a wild gesture towards the screens. "Out there, beyond the limits of Talamh, those ascended to the Light are free to do with it as they wish. The Haze exists only here, on Talamh. It is our protection. The Light cannot pierce it, cannot sense it. And so it has kept us safe all these years, free of human detection."

"That is why we came here, isn't it?" Serena asked. "You and the elders *looked* for this place, for a planet protected from their vision?"

A grimace crossed her father's lips. He met her eyes, and she saw a flicker there. A pain, or regret?

"Would that could have been the case," Aiden Levaanton replied, "but it is not. We did not come here alone, Serena." He turned to look at the humans. "I did lie to you, Rydian Holt. This planet was a savage wilderness when we came here, just as I told you. But there were no primitive humans, driven mad by the Haze. There was no one here at all."

"Then..."

"Your ancestors came to Talamh with the Alfur. They were renegades, men and women who decided they would rather control their own fate, than bow to their own human rulers. They freed a small group of Alfur and fled to the borders of the known universe. Fled in search of a planet on which they could call their own."

Her father paused to draw breath. His eyes scanned the room, taking in the slumped form of Jasmine, the wide eyes of the woman Hazel, the prowling figure of the great cat, and the brilliance that shone from Rydian. They settled finally on his daughter. On Serena.

"You did something to them, didn't you?" she whispered.

"No, Daughter. They did it to themselves."

TWENTY-SIX

Sand crackled and the air thrummed as Light burned across the stadium. The gathered forces of the Alfur shone as they too were unleashed, leaping forward to meet Bloodlust's power. The twin powers converged with a hiss and a boom that shook the Talamh beneath their feet. Wind swirled—then went rushing outwards before the force of the explosion.

Bloodlust stumbled as the world rocked. Cracks appeared amidst the sands as the floor of the stadium split apart. Sand swirled, disappearing down the freshly opened gaps. He had to leap aside as one opened close to his own feet.

The Alfur were not so lucky. They seemed to have come out worse off from the conflagration—every one of them had been knocked from their feet by the power of the blast. Several cracks had opened around them. Before it could react, one was swallowed up by the swirling sand, disappearing into the darkness beneath.

Four left, Bloodlust thought with a grin.

As the others struggled to find their footing on the thinning sand, he took up his greatsword once more. He paused a moment to search for Falcon, but the Goman champion was already on the move. True to her word, Falcon played by no rules. She was upon the creatures before they could fully recover.

Light bled from her skin as she struck, her gladius plunging down. Her victim cried out as it saw the blade descend and threw out its hand. Its Manus reader began to glow...then died to nothing as Falcon's blade plunged through the creature's throat, severing its spine. Its hand fell back to its side. With a shrug of her shoulders, Falcon let the Alfur fall.

Her sapphire eyes turned on the Alfur.

"Three to go," she said.

Roars carried down from the stands around them. The crowd had been silent, quelled since the appearance of the Alfurian ship. Cowards, cowering at the slightest show of strength. Now they emerged from their terror and saw that somehow, impossibly, their human champions held their own. Better even—three of the terrible Alfur were dead. Their enemy could bleed.

"Falcon, Falcon, Falcon!"

The cheers began as a whisper at first, but quickly they gathered force as the crowd came to their feet. Suddenly, anything was possible.

Bloodlust grated his teeth as their cheers carried down. A smile tugged at Falcon's lips as their eyes met. So far she had killed two and he had not even wet his blade. This was meant to be *his* challenge, *his* chance to test his strength. To strike down his enemies. Instead, Falcon had come to steal his glory.

"These three are mine," he snapped.

Bloodlust moved past Falcon before the woman could intervene further. He was cowering beneath the shawls of others. It burned him, who he had been before this day. How could he have allowed Rydian to fight in his place? How could he have stood by while the other Goman gladiators fought and died?

No more.

There were no smiles amongst the Alfur as they came for him this time. No snickers at these humans playing with their Light. They had seen the danger posed by these humans. They would not stop until Bloodlust rested in the dirt with his makers.

The Light in his veins had burned low from that last attack, but if his own stores were fading, surely these creatures must also be struggling. Grinning, he hefted his greatsword. Time to find out.

The three showed no sense of honour now. They came at him together, shining blades seeking human flesh. Bloodlust was not daunted. Here, finally, was a challenge worthy of his power, of his ability.

His greatsword caught the first attack on the flat of his blade—and this time he found his strength sufficient to meet the enemy's. He grinned, and pushed out, forcing the creature back. Light burned from his skin, casting back the shadows of the setting sun. In the distance, the first moon of Talamh had just peeked its emerald face above the walls of the stadium.

Bloodlust made to chase after his foe, but another Alfur stepped between them, even as the third went for his back. The pair struck in unison, seeking to pin him between their attack. He fed Light to his legs, granting them power, and sprung. Reinforced by the Light, the jump carried him over the head of the Alfur that had sought to thwart him.

As the pair struggled to disengage their blows behind him, Bloodlust landed beside the third creature. Surprise showed on its perfect face and it tried to raise its sword to counter, but either its Light was running low or it simply could not move in time. Bloodlust's greatsword clove through its chest in a bloody shower of bones and cartilage.

Then there were two.

Now it was his turn to grin as he turned to face the creatures. There was no arrogance in their faces now, no mocking laughter. Fear shone from their overly large eyes, but to their credit they did not back away. He could see the truth, the knowledge they were going to die. Strange, he hadn't thought the monsters had the spirit for courage.

It would not save them.

Red and white lit the world as Bloodlust summoned his power. His veins burned, but that fire no longer had the same sting. Something within was screaming, but Bloodlust savoured that burning.

Light gathered in his palm. The Alfur tensed, fists clenched, power gathering in their own Manus reader. It would not be enough, they knew. Not this time. Still they stood.

Raising his hand, Bloodlust unleashed his power. Finally the pair scattered, hurling themselves aside in a vain attempt to escape. One made it. The other did not. An inhuman cry rang through the arena as the Light caught the creature. For just a moment, the alien was lit by its glow, fixed in place, mouth stretched wide.

Then the screaming began.

Bloodlust watched with satisfaction as the beast's flesh began to boil. The translucent skin burned scarlet, then black, as fire consumed it from the inside out. Silver eyes burned away and the scream turned to a horrible gurgling.

And the Alfur fell to the sand, dead.

One more.

Bloodlust turned towards the cowering creature.

And his laughter rang from the arena walls.

TWENTY-SEVEN

Drums pounded in Rydian's ears. In his skull. In his blood and bones and flesh. His entire being vibrated with the Light he contained, his own, and what he had absorbed from Hazel.

Well, doesn't seem wise.

That was what the Alfurian prince had said. Rydian hadn't understood, but with each passing second, the pounding grew louder. The screams cut through his bond with Fatimah now, sliced a thousand cuts against his mind. It was worse still for the great cat. She sat still as a statue beside him, her every muscle, every limb straining.

The Haze was coming for them, its influence growing by the second, screaming for them to return to its grasps. Rydian wasn't sure how much longer they could last.

And the prince's words certainly weren't helping the situation.

"No, Daughter," the prince was saying. "They did it to themselves."

"What are you talking about?" he ground out the words between breaths.

"They were what we call scientists, your ancestors," Levaanton went on. "They studied natural phenomena—the Light most of all. But when they fled with their newly freed slaves, they knew their people could come for them. The human forces have seekers, members of their race whose Light has given them highly developed senses. They are capable of sniffing out renegades from a galaxy away. We needed a way to hide."

His voice was calm as he watched Rydian, and he sensed the prince understood his internal conflict. That he was waiting for Rydian to act, to crumble before the Haze. No doubt the Alfur outside would act then. Everyone in this room would perish. Teeth clenched, he redoubled his resolve.

"How?"

"Your people and ours worked side by side on a grand experiment."

The screens flickered, and he saw that his mother had raised her strange Manus reader again. She was controlling the flow of images. A picture of the twin moons of Talamh appeared on the largest screen.

"The Haze," Aiden Levaanton went on. "They thought they'd found a way to hide themselves from their own people. A way to hide an entire planet."

"But it didn't work," Rydian whispered.

"Oh it worked," the Alfurian prince said softly. "Their experiment sits in our skies even now, orbiting Talamh alongside its true moon, broadcasting its power across the planet. It just had...unintended side effects." His golden eyes swept over the room to settle on Rydian. "They were weaker than you, your ancestors. Let that give you comfort as the Haze takes your mind. It was only a few hours before the first began to crack."

"Why didn't they shut it off?" It was Hazel who spoke. She seemed to have regained some of her spirit now. "Why didn't they stop it?"

Aiden pursed his lips. "They tried."

Rydian's heart lurched. The shrieking in his mind redoubled in volume. A groan slipped from his lips as claws rent against his consciousness. He stumbled, and had to place a hand against the wall to keep himself upright.

"Oh yes, they tried," the prince continued. "Their measures had worked, cut us off from the universe. Not even our greatest instruments of the time could open a channel like these. We were safe." His cold eyes bored into Rydian's. "We could not allow them to doom us all."

"You...you..." Rydian couldn't get out the words. His knees gave way and he slumped to the ground.

"We did what was necessary," Aiden Levaanton rasped. He licked his lips, eyes turning to his daughter. "We drove back our human allies, kept them from these controls. Though it cost us greatly. Both Alfur and humanity were almost destroyed, but eventually we drove the humans into the jungles. There, the last of them finally succumbed to the Haze, to the madness they had brought upon themselves."

"That you...brought to them," Rydian panted.

Levaanton said nothing for a time. But finally he nodded. "Ay, we carried that guilt. It is why we built the Manus readers. A generation passed before they could be perfected. By the time humanity's minds were restored to them, all knowledge of the past had been lost. The council and I decided it was better that way, even amongst our own people."

"They...helped you," Rydian whispered. His vision was spinning now and his entire body was aflame. Looking up at the Alfurian prince standing over him, he saw the triumph in the creature's eyes. "What is...happening to me?"

"What happens to all your kind, eventually," Levaanton replied. "Your fortitude has impressed, but the Haze will not be denied."

"Father," that was Serena. Rydian's vision had closed in so much now he could not see the Alfur. "You said you would not hurt them. Please, we can be better than them. Let us find another way. Perhaps together, we can solve the Haze, free others..."

"You have seen his power," Levaanton voice remained calm as he addressed his daughter, but Rydian was watching the creature. He saw how the Alfur's fists clenched, the Light that shimmered beneath the translucent skin. "Imagine hundreds more like him. Thousands. The universe groans under the yolk of his kinds' power."

"Surely—"

"We are not people to them, Daughter," Levaanton crossed to Serena.

Rydian struggled to track them. A soft head lay in his lap and a rumble came from Fatimah. He wanted to comfort the beast, but all his concentration now was on the burning, on the screaming and the pain.

Give up, a thousand voices seemed to shriek. *Embrace us!* They demanded.

Somehow, Rydian took another breath, and held on.

"We are animals to them," Levaanton was saying. "Beasts of burden to be herded, marshalled, corralled, made to serve their wishes. We will never make them see us as equals."

"Sure not all of them..." Serena was still arguing on their behalf, but even to Rydian's ears, he could hear her resolve wavering. The images continued to play across the screens, the scenes of death and suffering. "Those who freed you and came here, they worked to protect us."

"They thought themselves our saviours," Levaanton practically spat the words. "That we owed them everything. They were not better than the others, only more sanctimonious..."

Suddenly, Rydian's mother was at his side, distracting him from the Alfur's words. He flinched as her face appeared next to him, cutting off his vision of the others. Her eyes were wide with fear as she looked down on him.

"Oh Rydian," she whispered. "What has this world done to you..."

"Mom..." He could barely think, barely breathe from the pain.

The voices buzzed, pressing at his mind, calling to his rage. The Alfur had done this. Finally, his deepest suspicions were confirmed. That the Haze was not natural. That the Alfur had known, could have stopped it, could have freed them all. But they had chosen not to. Chosen to save their own skins...

"Here, please, take this, Rydian. It will help."

Rydian forced himself to pay attention to his surroundings. To his mother. Blinking back the stars in his eyes, he struggled to make out what she held in her hand.

It was another Manus reader.

His racing heart froze. The world stood still. The Haze hadn't taken him yet. Restoring her device had protected Falcon for many more years, allowed her to... survive. He could save himself, escape the ravaging of the Haze.

But in doing so, he would be giving up the power to change their fate. To finally put a stop to the Alfur. To this place...

"No." The voice rang through the chamber. Footsteps approached, and a slender boot kicked the device from his mother's hand. She cried out, but a glare from Aiden Levaanton froze her in place. "It is too late for that. He has chosen his fate."

"No, you said he would be protected!"

"I am sorry, Jasmine Holt." There seemed to be genuine regret in the Alfur's voice now. "He is already too far gone."

Rydian knew it was true. His skull felt like it must be about to crack apart with the Light crammed within. His every muscle was locked like stone, else he would have thrashed as the fires lashed his every nerve, every sense.

"The time has come for mercy," Levaanton continued. The Alfur placed a pale hand on his mother's shoulder. "He must be put down, or we risk losing everything."

Those last words were like a bell tolling within Rydian. Within Fatimah too. He sensed the great cat grow tense, the Light within her suddenly blossom into life. It flared within him too. And with it, the defences of their minds finally burst asunder. A fresh force poured in through the breach, that surging, terrible anger, that rage he had barely held in check before their bond, before their freedom.

Now all was swept back before its power.

Like a drowning man, Rydian cried out a warning with his last breath.

TWENTY-EIGHT

Hazel could barely understand what was happening. She couldn't even tear her eyes from the screens. Scene after scene, she watched the Alfur fall, watched men and women like her beat them down. Some they crushed with their Light, others with fist and boot and blade. Bloody, terrible scenes all of them.

It was glorious.

Now if only they could help free her and Rydian and all the other humans on this planet...

"He must be put down, or we risk losing everything."

Her head snapped up, eyes focusing on the Alfurian prince. He loomed over Rydian, who lay sprawled on the floor. The treacherous creature, Jasmine Holt, crouched alongside him. Pretending she cared.

"Please, no." Her words whispered in the brightly lit room.

But what use was pleading with these creatures? Boots

thumped on stones as the creatures in the corridor filed inside, Manus readers at the ready.

No, the Alfur had shown their true colours, revealed the depths of their cruelty. It had been they who had destroyed humanity on Talamh, who had stolen their minds and their power—only to offer back their minds with chains attached. Little wonder they wished to remain hidden. When Hazel's relatives off-world discovered what they'd done here...

First we have to survive.

She clenched a bloody fist. Jasmine had bound her power, freeing her from the Haze, but denying her a chance to fight back. Serena stood beside her father, eyes filled with doubt, frozen. Little surprise there. Rotin had always been destined to betray them. Jasmine though...

Hazel frowned. The woman seemed to be in pain. Her face was clenched tight, wrinkles creasing the edges of her eyes as she clung to her son. If Hazel hadn't known any better, hadn't seen her callously murder her brother and so many others from the resistance...she would have said that Jasmine Holt truly cared about the fate of her son.

Good, the thought was an unworthy one, a shimmering remnant of the rage that had fuelled her through the long months after her brother's death. That rage had driven her to attack Rydian, to hold him to account for his mother's crimes.

Now though...now Rydian had done all in his power to help her, to aid humanity's plight, to defeat the Alfur. He didn't deserve to perish, to have the Haze wash away all he was, all he could be. Whatever pain it might cause Jasmine Holt.

"I trust this task to you, Daughter," the Alfurian prince was saying. "Prove to me you finally understand, that you are ready to take my mantle. The Alfur must stand united against the coming threats. There is no more room for division. One slip, one mistake, is all it will take for those beyond the Haze to discover us. Then there will be no future for any of us."

"Father..."

Hazel could see the indecision writ across Serena's face. She had little doubt which side the Alfur would choose in the end though. Blood always ran true. She would choose her own people. Choose to kill them all.

"You would trade our future for your own," Hazel whispered. She had to buy time, distract them long enough for Rydian to recover. She laughed, the sound harsh, raw. "Funny, you cannot see the irony, can you? All this time, your kind have treated us no better than animals. Even now you pretend *this* is a gift." She held up her hand, and blood still stained the device there. "But it is only another chain around our necks..."

The prince looked with derision in his eyes. "Your people had a thousand chances to be something more, to rise above your inherent nature. You have chosen violence every time."

"Chosen? You enslaved us! What else would we have chosen!"

"We did what had to be done. Your ancestors wrought

terrible damage in their madness. They forced us to take steps to ensure such events were never repeated."

"Steps? Steps like murder and genocide?" she snarled. "How is it humanity who chose violence, when every way I turn, it is *you* who are killing *us*?"

Her voice broke. Suddenly exhausted, she slumped against the wall. She wanted to fight and scream and pound these creatures into the ground, but what was the point? Rydian was crumbling. Johanas was probably already dead. Their last hope had proven false. What else was there to live for?

Revenge.

She supposed that would be something. If at least she could see the Alfur humbled, their crimes punished, she would go to her grave gladly. But even that power had been denied her.

"Bastards," she whispered.

To Hazel's- surprise, Serena met her eyes. "At least...at least you are alive," the Alfur whispered. "At least...we have treated you better than those sorry souls." Even as she spoke, her eyes slid away, as though her guilt would not allow her to hold Hazel's gaze.

"And yet our people suffer and starve and die. Every day. For your freedom."

"At least..." The Alfur's eyes were on the floor now. A tear streaked her cheek, but with a sudden shake of her head, she turned to her father. "I am sorry, Father. You were right. This system, I see now, I see why it was the only way."

Hazel had expected it, yet the Alfur's final betrayal was another barb to her heart. She stared at the pair, her insides hollowed out, her every hope drained away. Hatred pulsed within, and rage, but even the true, potent fury of the Haze was denied to her now. Lucky for these sorry creatures—she would have embraced its oblivion with open arms.

"He does not have long," Aiden Levaanton said quietly, looking from his daughter to Rydian. "Do it now, before he dooms us all."

A groan came from Rydian, and it seemed to Hazel that his flesh was burning brighter than ever with Light. But his eyes remained closed, and he did not react to their words. He lay on the floor, fingers clenched like claws, lips parted in a silent scream.

Serena's face tightened. Light began to stream from her Manus reader as she clenched her fist.

"It doesn't have to be this way," Hazel tried one last time. "He doesn't have to die. You can save him."

Serena paused. Her great golden eyes looked from Rydian to Hazel. There was pain there. This wasn't what she wanted. But finally they scrunched closed.

"No." She shook her head. "This is the only way. The only way my people stay free."

Hazel swallowed. "I wasn't talking to you."

The pair of Alfur stared at her, faces creased with confusion. A smile touched Hazel's lips. Maybe she would get her vengeance after all.

By the time understanding dawned in their eyes, it was already too late.

Behind them, Jasmine Holt, traitor of humanity, raised Hazel's blade high.

And drove it down through the mechanisms attached to the screens of Light.

TWENTY-NINE

Rage. Death. Destruction.

That was all there was now. Only the Light. Only the pounding of his rage, the roar of battle.

Johanas was long gone. Even Bloodlust was fading into the voices, into the screaming.

Until all that was left was the Haze.

Its power had swelled and grown, strengthened by the warring humans, by their own rage, their own hatred. Not even the devices of the vile Alfur could stop them now. Could prevent them from this victory.

All across the city, the men and women of Goma fought and died and emerged victorious. The arena had been cracked open, the raging crowds unleashed upon unsuspecting Enforcers. Nowhere was an Alfur to be seen. They had fled back to their towers, to cower there, waiting for the humans to come for them.

And come they would, Bloodlust knew.

The very air thrummed with their Light, tasted of their strength, burned with their power. None could escape them, not now. Not as one by one they threw off their shackles, broke free of their overlord's bonds...

Boom!

An explosion rocked the city, shook the very ground beneath their feet. Men and women stumbled— then were thrust to the ground by a wave of tumultuous air. Light blinded. Thunder deafened. Chaos reigned.

When the stillness finally returned, the men and women of Goma rose again under the stillness of night. Johanas rose with them, his mind a swirling vortex, his memories distorted, his world confused. But somehow, he was himself again. The whirling rage, the all-consuming hatred, all of it had vanished, as though it had never been. He clenched a fist, and the Light still came to him, seeping from his skin.

But the Haze was gone.

Though looking around, he saw that it was not without cost. Men and women lay dead all around him, while others moaned and struggled to rise, their injuries terrible to behold.

Johanas clenched his jaw. He could barely recall the details of the last few hours. But he knew that he had committed terrible acts. That some amongst the injured were his own victims. It didn't matter that they might have been Enforcers, that they might have threatened him. They were his responsibility.

Light spilt from his fingers and he moved to the nearest of the injured.

It was time he put his powers to a better use.

Morning found Johanas still at work. A larger party had joined him, of former gladiators and those who had witnessed his miracles and somehow found the powers within them. They had worked through the night to save who they could.

But as the sun rose slowly above the horizon, a stillness came over the group. Over the city. Johanas was the last to notice the change. Finally though, the whispers alerted him that something was wrong. That something had changed.

Turning, he followed the eyes of his companions upwards. The sky stretched overhead, shimmering with the brilliance of the sun. Shining a bright, vivid blue.

THE ROOM WAS SILENT AS RYDIAN RETURNED TO himself. He had clung on in the darkness, holding tight to his core, to himself. Somehow, he had held the Haze at bay. But even as he'd fought, he'd known this was a battle he could not win, that each moment of defiance bought only one more moment of sanity.

So how then did he find himself now at peace?

Blinking, he looked up from the floor. Serena and Prince Levaanton stood over them. He was surprised to see the horror on their faces, and for a moment he thought perhaps he *had* lost control. But no. They weren't looking at him.

Following their gaze, he found his mother standing over the ruins of some kind of unfamiliar machinery. Her face was pale, her eyes haunted as she faced the two Alfur.

"I told you," she gasped. "I told you he was not to be harmed."

The Alfur only stared, their faces bright with Light. Rydian struggled to understand what his mother had done. Even Hazel was staring, as though she couldn't quite believe what she'd witnessed.

And how had the Haze left him? Even as he sat on the floor, Rydian could feel the Light within him. It no longer burned, no longer lashed his spirit with that fiery pain. His mind was silent—but for his bond with Fatimah. Through it, he felt a similar confusion from the big cat, that it found itself suddenly free from a lifetime of torment. But...how was any of this possible?

Unless...

"Hello?"

Every soul in the room jumped as a crackling voice spoke suddenly from the machines Jasmine had not destroyed. The Light screens began to flicker, then one by one the images changed, until they all displayed the same thing. A human's face stared from each one. Rydian had the unnerving sensation that the man was looking at them.

"Hello, is that...Talamh?" Wrinkles creased the man's face as he squinted. "By the stars, how...there's...*captain*, you'd better come quick. I think we've got a code alpha."

There was a moment of silence in the chamber. They all looked at each other. Anguish was written across his mother's face, fear across those of the Alfur. Hazel's eyes shone with triumph.

Then from every inch of the room, alarms began to ring. And the voice came again.

"I repeat, code red, code red. All squadrons to sector 5.4: Talamh. Weapons hot. We've got an Alfur uprising to put down, boys."

Find out what happens next in Conquest and don't forget to leave a review.

NOTE FROM THE AUTHOR

If you've made it this far, thank you! This series is quite a different experiment for me, mixing a bit of science fiction, a bit of magic, a bit of spaceship stuff - and will be even more so with the third and final book! I also wanted to try and make them shorter, sharper books as well. So all and all quite different really, but hopefully the results have been enjoyable enough!

If not, I've got loots of much longer books and series for the avid reader of fantasy ;-)
Write on!
Aaron Hodges

FOLLOW AARON HODGES

Join Aaron Hodges on his newsletter to r**eceive TWO FREE novels and a short story!**
https://aaronhodgesauthor.com/newsletter

Book 1: Warbringer

Book 2: Wrath of the Forgotten

Book 3: Age of Gods

Book 4: Dreams of Fury

The Alfurian Chronicles

Book 1: Defiant

Book 2: Guardian

Book 3: Conquest

The Swords of Heaven and Hell

Book 1: Darkstrider

The Four Circles

Book 1: Help! My Wizard Mentor Had A Heart Attack And Now I'm Being Chased By A Horde Of Giant Spiders!

The Untamed Isles

The Path Awakens